Skyfall

by Phania Lee

Skyfall

by Phania Lee

ISBN 13: 978-1-955338-31-8

Cover elements, Canva, @mrrashad, @enola99d, @valeriimingirov, Wikimedia images, @ Rudez Studio from Rumah Kita, @Ciker-Free-Vector-Images from pixabay, @Adelia, @D-Stocks, and @DAPA images. Design by Lori Graham (Pocahontas Press).

Printed in the United States of America.

POCAHONTAS PRESS

Floyd, VA
pocahontaspress.com

Dedication

To my girls, Maia, Sidney, and Alyssa.

Chapter One

He was eleven when the Chautauqua came to town, a mud-show production whose gaudy playbill promised esteemed orators to breathe life into the roles of Shakespearean dramas, the epic tales of Homer. The Chautauqua, his older brother opined, offered educational entertainment second only to the profound messages found in the Scriptures.

So the boy tagged along, a shy, sensitive boy who thought himself a loner. He was mostly content with solitary pursuits such as fishing in the Little River, where he dangled a line from the riverbank for hours and watched the changing faces of clouds roll by.

But he soon grew impatient with the actors, their musty costumes and theatrical gestures. Though he listened to the poetry for its beautiful music, he longed to be outside with his dogs in the cool of an evening, lying on his back in a meadow under the summer constellations.

His brother warned that he'd never amount to anything without applying himself to practical matters. Already the family's old women whispered how the boy was touched by the year he was born, the fateful year of 1865 when the Confederates surrendered at Appomattox and President Lincoln was assassinated.

The boy heard the frenzy in the aunts' talk about God and the Devil, so why shouldn't they believe in Fate?

For the next act of the Chautauqua, two performers delivered a dramatic reading on the make-shift stage beneath the tent. He sat beside his brother and tried not to squirm, wondering if it would ever end, anxious for the final act.

With much mystery and fanfare, in flowing black robes covered by crescent moons and shooting comets, Ming the Magician emerged from a puff of smoke. He connected dozens of brass rings, released a dove from a hat to flutter over the heads of the audience, making the women squeal.

A chirping yellow canary in a gilded cage was held up before their eyes, and with a stroke of the magician's wand, both bird and cage vanished into thin air. To polite applause, Ming took a bow and left the stage.

As the crowd dispersed, the boy held back, yearning for more tricks, mesmerized by the magician's feats. Magic had put new thoughts into his head. His brother went to collect their transport, and together they rode home in the horse-drawn buggy.

He couldn't forget Ming's Magic Act. But the volumes in his father's library were on law and the Constitution, nothing about magic and wonder, and he soon despaired of discovering how the magician's tricks were executed. Now he had something new to ponder from the banks of the Little River, in the meadow at twilight while naming the stars.

In July, bright posters appeared on whitewashed walls of the feed store, in the window of the apothecary, tacked to locust posts at the livery stable. The circus would come to town in two days!

The weekly *Monitor* reported the circus itinerary, traveling by rail on its way from West Virginia to Roanoke, through Lynchburg and Charlottesville, then on to Richmond. The circus would stop in Wilson for a single day.

The boy begged his brother for the price of admission. A foolish enterprise, the circus, his brother said.

On a hot July day, the boy raked hay in a neighbor's barn until he was drenched with sweat and his flesh prickled, to earn the money for himself.

A clown doled out free tickets on the courthouse square to the lucky few. The boy teetered at the edge of the planked sidewalk along Main Street and heard the piercing whistles of the steam calliope heralding the parade.

A man on stilts fronted the procession, followed by the smallest man the boy had ever seen, with a head too big for his body.

Circus people in brilliant costumes led camels and little dogs, women in spangled bathing suits with ostrich plumes in their hair rode by on sleek Arabian ponies.

Clowns tossed peanuts to the crowd of spectators lining the street. Huge red wagons painted with gold designs carried lions and monkeys, and last were the elephants announced by the circus barker as The World's Most Prestigious and Prodigious Pachyderms.

The boy sprinted with other boys to the circus grounds on the outskirts of town, where they'd camped since dawn to watch the roustabouts hoist tents around the main poles lifted by the elephant's trunk. People hurried to the ticket booth, where they read the Program of Displays.

An African snake known to swallow a man whole!

Freaks of nature, oddities of the universe!

Wire-dancers – death-defying, spine-tingling!

Arcane Curiosities and Prestidigitation!

Ming the Magician had spoken the word, the boy remembered it for the way the syllables rolled off his own tongue – Prestidigitation. It meant *magic!*

He paid his coppers and rushed into the tent, enchanted by the mingled smells of sawdust and wild animals. After the lion tamer and the trick bareback riders, the clown show and the elephant walk, the acrobats and jugglers, the gas lights were dimmed.

To a dramatic drum roll, Horace Kellerman mounted center stage.

Seeking a volunteer from the audience, he chose a pretty girl with yellow hair.

"I must request absolute silence," the man said in a deep, impressive voice. "This feat of legerdemain requires total concentration."

As the boy watched in rapt fascination, the girl reclined on a table and, with a few mumbled words from the magician, rose horizontally into the air.

"Ethereal Suspension, ladies and gentlemen!" the magician declared, and the audience clapped wildly.

Horace Kellerman began to leave the stage, the girl still floating in suspension. But then he snapped his fingers and said, "Oh, yes! It slipped my mind!"

More magic words, and gently the girl drifted to the table and sat up, rubbing her eyes as if she'd been asleep during the entire procedure.

Cheers and whistles accompanied the magician to the wings.
The boy dashed from the tent, where he found the magician talking
and laughing with a woman dressed in the costume of the wire-dancing
troupe.

"Mr. Kellerman?"

The man turned around and looked down at the boy. But for his
stage make-up, he seemed like any man who lived in Wilson and worked
in town and wore a fine suit of clothes.

"Yes, I'm Horace Kellerman. What can I do for you, lad?"

"I...I wondered whether ethereal suspension is a trick, or if it
happened like you said."

Kellerman tousled the boy's hair with a white-gloved hand.

"Which would you rather have it be?"

"Can people really levitate?"

"They do in India and faraway places as a matter of course. Why,
the fakirs think nothing of it. That's f-a-k-i-r, son. Look it up."

Kellerman reached into his pocket and removed a small wooden
box. "Here. This is truly a trick for astonishing your friends." He opened
the box to reveal a coin. When he closed the box and opened it again, the
coin was gone. The magician blew on the box and handed it to the boy.

"Thank you, Sir!" The boy tried the trick several times, for the
coin to vanish and to reappear.

"Interested in magic, are you? Then allow me to furnish you with
a phrase which, should you divine its meaning, is guaranteed to keep you
interested in magic for the rest of your natural days."

The boy noticed as the wire-dancing woman gently pulled the
magician away, though she watched the boy with a smile.

"Remember what I'm about to disclose to you, son, and remember
it well. The phrase is this: the astral body projected into etheric realms."

"The astral body..."

"Projected into etheric realms."

Then the man whose name he would never forget, Horace
Kellerman, strolled away with the wire-dancer, her graceful white hand
with red-lacquered nails arranged on the arm of the magician's black
coat.

The boy took the coin-trick home and amazed his brother. But the words the magician shared with him he revealed to no one, a secret whose meaning he was determined to discover, however long it might take, whatever the sacrifice.

When the circus left town that Fourth of July, he was no longer the same boy.

At the age of eleven he'd been given a dream.

The year was 1876.

****

Meg Kites had been in her new house for four months, the first time she tried to convince herself that she could not have seen the man who wasn't there.

At age fifty, after two daughters, a divorce, and a death, Meg had purchased the first house of her very own with the hope that it would become her sanctuary. But it was a notion profoundly disturbed by a fleeting vision in her headlights, when the apparition materialized in the center of a country road on a foggy morning as sunrise began to gray the sky.

The morning in late September began abnormally enough, when Jenny came into her mother's bedroom at three-thirty a.m. "Mom? It's time to wake up."

"Okay, okay." Meg tried to pry her eyes open. She moved her feet from the snug womb of the goose-down comforter, displacing one of the cats who slept at the foot of her bed on his own pillow. She looked down at Cappy, her black fluff, distinguished by his purr that sounded like a throaty chortle.

The coffee pot had been set to brew last night before Meg's vain attempt to fall asleep at nine. She pulled a housecoat over her night-gown and sat at the kitchen table with a cup of black coffee to ruminate about the coming day. She hadn't slept well last night, tendrils of the past creeping from her subconscious to ensure hours of tossing and turning, persistent memories best left forgotten.

Jenny entered the kitchen in her perky fast-food uniform, brushing her long chestnut hair with a boar-bristle brush. "Are you sure you won't fall asleep at the wheel?"

"You sound like a TV ad on the perils of drunk driving," Meg said with a cavernous yawn. "I'll be alert once I've had my coffee."

"Maybe you should have a second cup before we leave."

Wryly, Meg said, "You're such a considerate child."

After graduating from Wilson County High School in June, Jenny had just celebrated her eighteenth birthday. For two months she'd been working the drive-through window of the locally infamous Burger Master, a new restaurant recently constructed in their town despite much protest from the old-timers allergic to change.

Meg was inclined to give her daughter credit, with so many of Jenny's friends sitting around on their duffs, by day spending their parents' money at the Blue Ridge Mall and running around all night to parties. But Jack, Jenny's father who thankfully lived five hundred miles away, had been horrified by his youngest daughter's decision to wait a year before entering college.

"Why should I go to college," she'd written in a letter to her father, "when I don't have any idea of what I want to become?"

By inevitable comparison, Jenny's older sister Claire had traipsed off to college a year early, finished in three years, and now had a lucrative, demanding job as a retail buyer for a major clothing chain in Maryland.

But Claire was ten years older, and Meg had been a different mother with each child. Claire had the benefit of Meg's youthful, energetic years, while Jenny received the patience and relative wisdom of an older, seasoned mother.

And her daughters' lives had been different, too. Meg hadn't found the courage to divorce Jack until Jenny was fourteen. But both daughters had learned by their mother's example to keep rolling along and never give up, despite life's kaleidoscopic offerings. Or so Meg comforted herself at those times she suspected she'd failed her children miserably, by finally ending a destructive marriage and asserting her own independence.

"Are you ready yet?" Meg called with another yawn.

"If you'll braid my hair!"

Together they walked to Meg's ten-year-old Renault parked in the front yard. Rain had slicked the blacktop road leading to the main highway, a middle-of-the-night autumn rain. Only the steady drone of crickets filled the pre-dawn silence.

They lived a few miles off the beaten track, with several houses spaced along the road. Having grown up in a suburb of Chicago, there were times when Meg felt completely isolated, which suited her fine. The days at her office provided more than enough in the way of human interaction.

She and Jenny had lived in the little white house with their animals since May, but Meg still hadn't done much more than wave at her neighbors in passing, usually when driving to or from her job. Every community has its own protocol, and country people seem inclined to give a wide berth to their neighbors' affairs.

As Meg started the car and backed out of the driveway, Jenny said, "You will call around to see if somebody can fix my car, won't you?"

"Of course. A promise made is a debt unpaid."

"But please tell them it has to be fixed fast, Mom. I don't want to be stranded this weekend."

Heaven forbid, Meg thought to herself, but didn't say. Jenny had yet to learn about auto mechanics repairing vehicles at their own speed, and how no amount of hassling could expedite matters. Nor was there any method for predicting what the bill might be. Forget estimates; they were a joke. These realities were compounded by the fact that Jenny's car was an old Mazda RX7, and few mechanics in the area could be trusted to work on a rotary engine.

It was a mere three-mile drive from their house to the restaurant, down a winding road where deer or raccoon might lope out innocently to the highway cutting through the sleepy town. Meg had lived in three different parts of Virginia, but it was here in the Blue Ridge range of the Appalachians where she'd come to feel most at home.

Gemini: air, mountains. Or was there any truth to the Zodiac?

She wouldn't have wanted to move back to Richmond or to

Northern Virginia even with the lure of an exorbitant salary, and there had been a few offers several years ago. But by then she'd been in the thick of a bitter divorce from Jack Kites.

Now, she was not sorry for the decisions and choices she'd made. Early on, living with Jack's incessantly self-centered demands, she had become intimately acquainted with the concept of Overload. A human organism, regardless of how tough, could handle just so much stress and still manage to be reasonably functional. When Claire told her Jack had been dating a woman in whom he'd been interested, who suddenly said she never wanted to see him again because he was too controlling, Meg didn't feel vindicated, only sad. Though she didn't love him anymore, she bore him no malice.

"It's kind of nice being up before the birds, isn't it?" she said to Jenny. "The world seems so fresh and clean without people hurrying about."

"I like getting up at three a.m."

"Oh, I really believe that!"

"No, I do, Mom. Then I have the afternoons to spend time with my friends. Of course in the winter, it will probably be different. Everybody will be working or away to college."

"Which is where your little fanny will be, next fall, and I don't care what you decide to major in. Deal?"

"Deal."

Meg stopped for the red traffic light. The Wilson Chamber of Commerce tourist brochures boasted one traffic light in the entire county, and this was it. The only cars in sight were the two parked in the restaurant parking lot belonging to the manager and another early-morning shift worker greatly admired by her Burger Master peers as the biscuit maker.

"Bye, Mom. Try to go back to sleep if you can."

"Call me at the office before five and let me know when to pick you up, if someone else can't give you a lift."

Today Jenny would work four hours, and then she and three other women were driving to the Burger Master home offices in North Carolina for a training session intended for new service coordinators. It meant a thirty-cent per hour raise.

Meg drove home, turned off the lights, and told the cats to go back to sleep as it wasn't yet time for breakfast. She settled under the covers with Cappy on his pillow at her feet and had almost dozed off when grating rings of the telephone sliced through her drowsiness.

She groped for the bedroom door but couldn't find the doorknob in the dark, nor could she seem to locate the light switch. Irritated, she stumbled through the bedroom doorway after conking her head on the edge of the open door and yanked the receiver from the wall phone.

"Mom? Could you please find my other work shirt and see if my name badge is on it?"

Jenny. Of course, who else would it be at four a.m.? Once upon a time it could have been Warren, feeling lonely and maudlin on one of his all-night benders, but not any longer.

"Hang on a minute, I'll look." The shirt was crumpled on the floor of Jenny's bedroom with the badge still anchored to the right pocket. Meg went back to the phone. "It's here. I'll drive it up to you."

"Are you sure, Mom?"

Was she sure? Then why else had Jenny called? She couldn't very well go to Burger Master Headquarters in North Carolina without her name badge fastened proudly to her chest.

"I'll be right there. Look for me and run out to the car. As you know, I'm not properly attired to come in."

Once again, the cats were instantly alert, churning around her ankles like soft, elegant fur stoles. "Be home in a minute, guys. Then I'll feed you."

She threw a raincoat over her nightgown, grabbed her purse and car keys, jammed her feet into Earth Shoe sandals, and made the return trip.

Jenny waited at the curb. "I'm really sorry, Mom."

"An understandable oversight. I'll survive. Be sure and try to get some fun out of the day. I'll talk with you later."

"Oh, it's going to be a laugh a minute. Two of the women I'm riding with aren't even on speaking terms."

The sky was still black, vestiges of rain clouds illuminated by an occasional light penetrating the darkness along the highway. No traffic traveled in either direction. Meg turned off the highway onto Rural Route 862 leading to her house and drove into thick, patchy fog.

She downshifted into second gear to make the turn, then slapped the gearshift into third. Watching for meandering animals, she clicked on the high beams of her headlights which only made the fog worse, so she lowered the beams.

After the first curve rounding a hill, she accelerated into fourth, idly wondering what she would do after feeding the cats. If she ran the vacuum cleaner at this hour, she'd feel as though she had died and gone to housecleaning hell.

She might as well brew another pot of coffee. She could always work on her knitting and search for a decent movie on HBO. Sleeping wasn't an option, now that she was wide-awake. Well, she'd just go to bed early tonight, to make up for last night's insomnia.

She could almost drive this road by rote, as the curves and dips had mapped themselves into a mental pattern. With the window cracked open, she heard the cattle lowing in nearby pastures. Abutting her back-yard was a hilly meadow where cows and young bulls grazed around an old abandoned house made of hand-hewn logs.

It was true that her house had been less expensive than she'd anticipated, but only because it had remained vacant for a number of years and needed major renovation. Ned Roanes, the jocular real estate agent, had told Meg that a ninety-seven-year-old widow died in her house. Then the woman's daughter had lived in the house until she became ill. Several years later a couple of newlyweds bought it and stayed a few weeks before putting it back on the market. Though Meg pressed him, the agent couldn't seem to recall exactly how long the house had been vacant.

"But why did the young couple move out so quickly?" she asked.

"Beats me. Maybe they were having marital troubles. Then again, some of us folks below the Mason-Dixon Line feel funny about living in a house where somebody died."

"How odd, and what a silly superstition, isn't it? Fifty years ago, nearly everyone died at home. Breathing one's last breath in the

Intensive Care Unit is a fairly modern convenience."

"Glad you feel that way, Mrs. Kites," Ned replied with a grin, revealing several spaces where molars should have been. "But you have to appreciate the local customs around these parts, if you're going to be hobnobbin' with the natives. It doesn't matter if somebody had a coronary on the front steps, just as long as a former resident didn't draw his last breath, as you put it, inside the front door. Why, I've even known of families who dragged Granddaddy's corpse out to the barn and said he keeled over while milking the cows instead of peacefully passing away in his own bed."

"Ned, you're such a clown."

"It's the gospel truth, Mrs. Kites. But death or no death, this is a little sweetheart of a home for you and your daughter. With just a bit of fixing up."

"Well, exactly what needs repair, Ned?"

"Oh, not much, I'm sure."

But at closing, after she had signed her name on the dotted lines, Meg learned firsthand how the buyer should beware when the seller doesn't dicker over the first offer, and clearly states the sale of the property is made *as is*.

Having the interior painted, half the roof reshingled, and the water pump repaired had run up the cost. But the selling point in Meg's mind, and what convinced her to buy, was the old log house with its red tin roof and ancient stone chimney that had survived to make its own history a few yards behind her backyard fence.

Surrounded by primrose, cedars, a holly tree and willows, the house boasted a crop of catnip along one side that was soon discovered by Meg's cats. Ned Roanes said he believed no one had lived there for many years, but the type of construction suggested the log house was more than a century old and "a prime example of Appalachian craftsmanship of yesteryear."

A boarded-up privy stood out back, where a large red squirrel had made a home and gathered black walnuts from an adjacent tree. Picturesque, quaint – Meg thought of dozens of words, yet none to adequately explain her fondness for the house.

Cattle were in the meadow infrequently, herded by a farmer in a brown pick-up truck to unseen pastures. There was a concrete water trough with green algae growing on the surface of the water and several fish below. Close by, an active spring flowed beside willow trees. From her own back porch, she had a clear view of the old log house, leading to a hilly, rolling meadow topped by a half-fringe of trees in the distance etched black against a dome of sky.

Meg felt that living in such a peaceful setting was well worth the commute to her job twenty-four miles each way. Had it not been for Jenny, she'd have seriously considered a townhouse close to her office. But Jenny still needed a home base, and Meg was determined not to uproot her youngest daughter from familiar friends and surroundings. They had been through too much turmoil and sadness in the past four years.

Stifling a yawn, Meg coasted around the final turn and involuntarily stomped the brakes, screeching to a wavering stop that seemed to pass from the car into her trembling legs.

Standing in the middle of the road was a tall, pale man with a black mustache clad in a black top hat and waistcoat.

Her initial alarm turned to anger. She had been so startled that her right foot released the accelerator and, before she could hit the clutch, the car stalled. She flung open the car door to jump out, prepared to hurl a few acidic remarks.

"What do you think you're doing!" she called to him. "I could have run over you!"

But as she watched, the figure began to dissolve, waning to a faint shadow and disappearing like so much vapor. Meg wondered if she *had* fallen asleep at the wheel, if it had been only a dream.

Shaking her head, she got back in the car, started the engine and slowly, cautiously drove the rest of the way home. She sat in the driveway for several long minutes, still quaking from the shock of the incident.

Had she seen a ghost? In her mature adult years, she had always been too practical to believe in ghosts, haunts, or spectral beings. But if it hadn't been a ghost, what alternative explanation could there have been for what she had witnessed?

An imprint from her subconscious mind, some image from a dream emerging from her own psyche? She had studied Jung's concept of the collective unconscious in college psychology, a theory claiming existence of images universally implanted in the human mind and cross-cutting all cultures.

Meg fed the cats, made a half pot of coffee and waited while it dripped through. When she poured a cup and added an ice cube, the cats were ready to go outside for their morning adventure. She propped open the screen door to the back porch and watched them scamper out, noting how the sky had turned a delicate lavender threaded with blue. The sunrise was coming early today.

She turned on the radio to the local country music station playing a hymn called *Stairway of Gold*, about how Jesus would save her soul. This was followed by s bluegrass instrumental featuring a merry banjo-picker, music to stay awake by. The announcer promised that today's featured artist between seven and eight a.m. would be Tanya Tucker.

Before she moved to this part of the state, Meg hadn't enjoyed any country music artist beyond Willie Nelson. But now she hummed along with the predictable tunes, amused and somehow cheered by the words that always rhymed and told the simple stories of decent people involved in the joys and heartaches of love, betrayal, and separation.

Meg sat down at the kitchen table with the message pad left there for Jenny to report her daily whereabouts to her mother. Yesterday's message read: "Mom, Carrie took me shopping for a couple of hours. See you soon! Love, Jenny."

She turned to a fresh sheet and wrote: *A man in black top hat and old-fashioned waistcoat.* What archetypal, Jungian image did that bring to mind?

An undertaker or mortician. Pall-bearer? A harbinger of death?

Annoyed with herself, Meg pushed the pad away, ripped off the top page and balled it up to toss into the wastebasket. Better stop with this nonsense while she is still ahead.

Today was going to be a bear, anyway. With few exceptions, Meg genuinely cared about her staff, and believed in the department's mission to render public service to those who were often victims of social injustice. But today she had to deal, finally, with a recalcitrant staff member, a man she had long suspected was mentally unbalanced. His strident, hostile, devious remarks had poisoned the work environment for everyone else in the office.

Meg knew she had let it go on for much too long. She didn't want to be heartless, but as the supervisor, she was paid to take care of such matters. Never mind that she faced an unpleasant task and would probably end up with a crushing migraine.

At her annual physical exam several months ago, her doctor had written a prescription for a mild tranquilizer to be used for the purpose of smoking cessation. Meg had filled the prescription, though she wasn't quite ready to relinquish her ten daily cigarettes, her last remaining vice. But this morning she planned to take a tranquilizer, with an assurance she'd need one simply to keep her wits during the impending, predictably nasty confrontation with the staff member she'd long thought of as the Bad Seed.

Calmly, she watched the sky brighten into a bona fide sunrise, listening as the birds sang a subdued September serenade. It promised to be the sort of gorgeous day that made you dread winter all the more. After a long, hot bath, she dressed, applied make-up and styled her hair.

For lunch, she packed low-fat yogurt, an apple, and a bagel. Really, she was going to have to lose fifteen pounds, or she would look exactly as she did now for the rest of her life, or maybe even worse.

She had put on the weight after Warren died, the man with whom she'd had an impetuous affair a year after Jack drove away. Warren had been in her life for more than a year, before he finally succeeded in completing a thirty-year project of drinking himself to death.

Sometimes she wondered if Jenny would ever forgive her mother for becoming involved in that doomed relationship. But at the time, despite her career in client services, Meg had somehow managed to fool herself into believing that she and Warren would grow old together and have a happy life. He had a dry sense of humor, he made her laugh, he said he loved her.

Funny, what loneliness could do. Though she'd learned to live with an extra fifteen pounds, she had come to the realization that, with one controlling manic-depressive and one suicidal alcoholic for a track record, Meg Kites was probably better served by a solitary life. Finding another man to share her autumn years was the last item on her personal agenda.

"You kids be good, and Grammy will see you tonight," she said to her cats, who looked at her in unison as if she had truly lost her marbles. She went to her car, backed out of the driveway, and drove up the road for the third time that morning.

As Meg approached the second curve, she wondered whether she would forever remember the image of the man frozen in her headlights on a September morning, only to vanish before her eyes.

Chapter Two

Meg downed her tranquilizer with a sip of hot coffee, inadvertently causing the pill to dissolve in her mouth before she could swallow it. In less than a minute, she felt woozy. The damned thing had gone right to her head.

Her knees felt weak. She sat at her desk, resting her face on her folded arms, and tried to collect her thoughts. How she hated the dizzy feeling of being out of control!

Having a cigarette entered her mind, but that meant she'd have to leave the office and skulk out to her car like the weak-willed pariah she was. With the Virginia GASP law, employees were no longer allowed to smoke in public buildings except in designated areas, and no smoking lounge for fostering staff camaraderie existed in the humble offices of the Department of Social Services. As underdog of the County government, they were lucky to have a miniscule kitchen.

The office chit-chat flowed into her cubicle from the next room where the coffee machine, refrigerator, and microwave were located, the topics of discussion having not the slightest connection with job duties or the business of public service.

But perhaps that was Meg's fault. She knew she was too lax, but she didn't believe in make-work, either. Why couldn't adults be depended upon to perform their jobs without a supervisor breathing down their necks?

Her policy of supervision was based on the Golden Rule: treat others as she wanted to be treated. Sometimes, when she observed the reality of Murphy's Law on an almost daily basis -- that if anything can go wrong, it will -- she caught herself marveling that she and her staff were actually paid salaries.

Once she'd had a young, spunky secretary with nothing to lose who said, "If you took all these jobs in here and rolled them together, you'd have one real job." Meg had to admit there was a lot of truth to the girl's observation.

But by far the worst part of supervision was dealing with the personal problems that interfered with even minimal job performance. In a nutshell, this was exactly the trouble with the Bad Seed, who had daily disruption down to a fine art.

Something was always awry in his pinched little life, usually two or three major crises at a time, no small feat for a confirmed bachelor without obligations to anyone but himself. Meg had made diligent efforts to have the Seed transferred to another department, but the man's reputation had spread countywide years ago, and no one else wanted to deal with him, either.

After she finished her coffee, Meg walked down the hall and knocked at the door of one of the few offices that had two windows, whose nameplate read Norman J. Feder, MSW, Senior Social Worker.

He lounged at his desk reading the morning newspaper.

"Well, hello, Meg. To what do I owe this auspicious visit from on high?" A greasy smile spread across his wizened face.

He'd meant it as a joke – *hadn't* he?

"Mister Feder, your annual performance evaluation is due next week, and I'm afraid we need to talk."

"Oh? About what?" The tone of voice was decidedly icy.

She ticked off a few of the milder complaints regarding his frequent absences and failure to meet basic job responsibilities in the past twelve months.

Mr. Feder's hackles went up. "I see," he said in a snappish tone. "Once again, you're hell-bent on trying to take my job away."

"Look at this from my point of view," Meg said gently. "Why would I want to do that? I'd have to advertise, recruit, and train someone new. I'm not in the mood to go through the rigmarole. Besides, you have years in the field to your credit. I'd much rather work with you, to make sure these objectives are finished on time. Is that so much to ask?"

In a huff, Mr. Feder folded the sections of the newspaper, taking his sweet time about it.

"I may as well inform you now, Miz Kites. I'm going to take a sick day tomorrow and be evaluated for antidepressant medication, and there's every possibility my physician will insist I take an extended medical absence to relieve myself of your unwarranted, unnecessarily stressful expectations. I'll have the leave slip on your desk for your signature promptly."

Meg felt her gorge rising, but evidently the tranquilizer had done its job, because she refrained from reminding the Bad Seed that he'd already been out with one thing or another nearly three months in the past fiscal year.

And due to his long tenure with the Department, he had accrued oodles of leave time, which meant he must be paid for the days he was off, regardless. The situation removed the possibility of hiring a temporary fill-in while he was away, which meant the other staff were forced to solve problems associated with his caseload and griped loudly to Meg about it.

No, Mr. Feder was not a popular man.

"Just keep me informed," she said with a smile and hurried back to her office, where she closed the door, sat at her desk, and buried her face in her hands.

Oh, *why* had she ever wanted to rise to the middle echelons of management in the bureaucracy? When her patience had been totally spent, the cockeyed laws of the universe expected her to come up with more, apparently a limitless supply where the Seed was concerned. It was difficult enough to show up every day without such problems. Were it not for the pressing reality of bills to pay, Meg didn't believe it would be worth it at any price.

From a long career in public service, her personal slogan was: it's too hard, doesn't pay enough, and nobody cares. There was a lot of truth in that, too.

She looked at her daily list of things to do, repetitive tasks she could finish blindfolded in twenty minutes. Her mode of operation included a philosophy of handling each piece of paper only one time, so that her In-box was always cleared.

An administrative management meeting had been scheduled for

noon. Meg went to the library at eleven, just to get out of the office. She browsed the new novels, but she'd read most of the interesting offerings months ago. She decided to look in the non-fiction stacks.

Unexplained Phenomena was on the shelf beside books on UFOs, Bigfoot, and near-death experiences, and she tucked it under her arm. In the racks of psychology and self-help selections, she found a basic reader on Jungian theory. She went to the desk to check out both books, walked to her car, threw the books in the back seat, and returned to the office.

As she walked down the corridor, Meg overheard the Seed making snide remarks in his office, telling several staff who happened to be in the vicinity and were willing to listen, how cruelly Meg had treated him. At the sight of Meg, the other staff scurried, allowing her to march into the Seed's office and close the door.

"I've had all of this I'm going to tolerate," she said. "If you have complaints or grievances, I want you to bring them directly to me, and we'll discuss it. If I overhear any more negative or self-pitying comments, or if other staff relate things to me you've said to them – and they do, you know – I'm going to write you up. Now, is that understood?"

"I don't know what I've done to make you hate me so! Tell me, please. What have I done?"

Surely he was joking again – *wasn't* he?

Meg couldn't trust herself to deal with this any further today. The tranquilizer had worn off, and she was afraid to open her mouth to utter another word. The Seed would file a lawsuit in a heartbeat. If he could have seen Meg run down by an Amtrak train, the Seed would have sold tickets. Such a thoroughly unpleasant, vindictive little man!

She merely said, quietly, "I've stated my position. Please try and remember it." Then she grabbed a notepad and pen and walked the four blocks to the County courthouse for her meeting, never mind that her ill-fitting, discount store leather-look plastic pumps rubbed blisters on her feet before she reached the doorstep.

Somehow she made it through the rest of the day, thinking as she drove home that, with the Seed out tomorrow, even if the work wasn't done, at least a temporary atmosphere of peace would prevail. Meg wished she had it within her feeble powers to pay Mr. Feder to stay home forever.

Jenny was feeding the cats when Meg came into the house. "Hi, Mom! I got a ride home. And guess what?"

"What? Tell me something wonderful. I need it." She hung her car keys on the special hook, put her purse on the piano, and reached up under her skirt to pull her pantyhose to her hips. Then she sat down in a kitchen chair, eased the pumps from her swollen feet, and began to remove the pantyhose that were stuck to the blisters.

"In six months, the general manager said I could apply for a college scholarship!"

"Well, wouldn't Jack adore that?" The divorce agreement stated that Jack would pay Jenny's tuition at a State university, while Meg shouldered the cost of books, clothing, health care, and living expenses. "For what kind of curriculum?"

"I don't know for sure. Business Management, I guess. But Mom, the manager rakes in forty thousand a year. Of course, she works a lot of hours and has all the responsibility."

"You can't sneeze at that, Jenny. It took me twenty years to make forty thousand."

"You just chose the wrong line of work. It's nice to want to help people, but not when society could care less. No offense, but you shouldn't have to work your whole life and have nothing to show for it."

"No argument there. But in your case, if you worked your way up to manager, by the time you're twenty-five you'd be tired of fast food. You might even smell like a human cheeseburger. But by then you'd have earned a college degree, so you could easily shift into a different field. A degree in business management would be applicable in many settings other than fast food."

"I didn't know you'd see it my way," Jenny said with a grin.

"You think I'm going to discourage you? It sounds smart to me, Jenny."

"Yes, but you wouldn't be very impressed with some of the people I work with, though."

"Believe me, after fifteen years with the Bad Seed, nothing could surprise me. You're going to find people like that no matter where you work or what field you're in, people who resent you because you're the boss, and take fiendish pleasure in plotting ways to sabotage your efforts. You learn how to work around them."

"Have you?"

"Nope," Meg admitted. "I'm still learning. Our talk today was, as always, a disaster."

"Well, Mom, he's just a really unhappy person."

"Tough! Why does he have to make everyone else pay the piper for his miserable life? Frankly, I'm sick to death of his constant whining."

"Think about it, Mom. It must be pretty humiliating for Mr. Feder to have been in the same job twenty years and keep getting passed over for a promotion."

"I know, Jenny. He applied for the director job when I did, and he's never gotten over it because I was hired and he wasn't even given an interview."

"Then you need to remember how he feels and have some sympathy for him."

"I have! I do! That doesn't work, either. He just wants more and more of it, like a bottomless suck-hole!"

She caught herself then, thinking of how she must sound to her youngest daughter. Some example *this* was.

But as she might have predicted, already Jenny's thoughts were elsewhere.

"Mom, did you have a chance to find out about my car?"

Meg related the finer points of what was wrong with the Mazda, and how much it would cost to have it repaired. Not a pleasant topic, but safer than dwelling on the Seed.

In her own home. On her time off.

Chapter Three

At last it was Saturday, Meg's day to sleep until eight o'clock instead of six-thirty. Unlike her work attitude Monday through Friday, she bounded from bed in a mood of reckless anticipation, yet another reminder of her continual yearning about retirement not coming soon enough.

Early autumn in Virginia, and she planned to take full advantage of another eighty-degree day. After being cooped up in a windowless office all week, Meg considered it a balm to her spirit, handling outdoor chores.

Yesterday Jenny had driven Meg's car to pick up Cherry Lamb from the vet. The fifteen-year-old Brittany Spaniel, with her nocturnal yelping and incontinence, was on her last legs, and a frequent visitor at Dr. Cole Mitchum's veterinary clinic.

Cherry Lamb, grateful to be home and yet fast becoming another bane of Meg's life, followed along with a hopeful expression on her graying face as Meg planted bulbs around the yard.

She looked across the fence at the old log house where Cappy methodically licked the dried blooms of the catnip. She had a few red tulip bulbs left and decided to dig them in along the side of the old house. Whoever planted the catnip must have been an animal lover, and Meg took pleasure in planting new flowers in the person's memory. It was such a forlorn little house, the flowers would make it seem more cheerful in the spring.

She wiped the dirt from her hands on the grass, then went around to the front of the house and climbed the locust-wood steps to the porch. Mud-dauber wasps had built their furrowed tubular nests on the underside of the porch ceiling and were buzzing lazily overhead. She cupped her hands on either side of her face and tried to peer inside through a crack in the indoor shutters, to no avail.

Meg stood on the porch for a few minutes longer gazing out over the meadow, imagining how the world had been a century ago in the eyes of the people who'd built this house. Her active imagination conjured several scenarios that she realized were probably gleaned from watching television episodes of *The Waltons* or *Little House on the Prairie*. She opened the screen door and tried the front doorknob. Locked, of course.

Bart, Cappy and Babu had been milling around the yard languidly, but suddenly bolted across the fence to their own territory. Meg followed, surprised when she noticed Cherry Lamb whimpering at the fence. That dog, old and doddering as she was, generally wanted to go anywhere at any time. Dutifully, Cherry trailed Meg into the house.

"Here, old gal. Have some breakfast." She placed her bowl of soggy shredded wheat on the floor near the dog's water bowl. Then she carried up the vacuum cleaner from the basement and attacked the floors, the country music station turned high so she could hear it over the drone of the machine.

Returning the vacuum cleaner to the basement, Meg noticed the basement stairs covered with a hairy growth. She read the back of the Clorox bottle, took the bucket, and went to the outside spigot to mix a mild solution of Clorox and water purported to remove the brown, matt-like fungus. Remembering the last time she'd seen the scrub brush was when she cleaned the bathroom, Meg went inside the house to get it.

She glanced at her face in the bathroom mirror, and how she was beginning to look as old as she sometimes felt. But she wasn't quite ready for the silver hair at her temples. At least a rinse could remedy that. Which still left the problem of the extra fifteen pounds, the cigarette habit, and a vague tracing of wrinkles earned over a lifetime and here to stay, although the expensive skin lotion she'd bought a few weeks ago seemed to be helping. She washed her hands and slathered more lotion on her face, taking special care with the crow's-feet at the corners of her eyes and the creases adorning the space between her eyebrows etched by years of frowning over mind-numbing paperwork. Taking the scrub brush from the cabinet under the bathroom sink, she went back outside to tackle the basement steps.

The bleach and water in the bucket she'd left on the top step had come to a boil, as surely as if it had been placed over high heat on the kitchen stove. Curious, Meg placed her hand over the steam. Boiling, but not hot. Gingerly, she poked a finger into the solution and realized it wasn't even warm. In fact, it felt ice-cold.

When she dropped the brush into it, the boiling stopped. Some strange chemical reaction, she guessed, perhaps from minerals in her well water. Finding an empty Mason jar, she scooped some of the liquid into it. She would ask the Extension Agent, whose office was above hers, about this on Monday.

Meg whiled away the afternoon moving potted plants into the house and basement for winter, washing sweaters and blouses, and hanging sheets and towels on the clothesline in the backyard to dry in an afternoon breeze. She wondered when Jenny would come home. Now that the Mazda was repaired, when Jenny wasn't at Burger Master she was either asleep or on the road. Meg envied her daughter's energy level.

Jenny bounced into the kitchen just as Meg assembled the ingredients for a pan of lasagna. "Hi, Mom. Nell's waiting in the car, we're going shopping, but I need to talk with you. It's important."

"I'm listening."

"Not right now, I have to go. Maybe tomorrow? I'm staying at Nell's tonight, if it's alright with you."

"Okay, but could you do me a favor?"

Jenny stripped off her uniform, draping shirt, trousers, and black socks over the back of a kitchen chair. She pulled on a pair of shorts and a cotton blouse. "I guess so, but we're in a hurry."

"Can you run up to the store and bring back a big carton of low-fat cottage cheese? I want to make lasagna but forgot to buy cottage cheese."

"Oh, good. Save some for me. But I'll need money. I haven't cashed my check yet, and the bank's closed."

"Take a twenty from my wallet. And bring me a six-pack of diet cola."

"Be back in a flash"

"You can keep the change."

"Thanks, Mom."

Meg glanced out the kitchen window as Jenny ran to the Mazda and hopped into the sporty chariot that had set Meg back nearly three-thousand dollars last August. But as she had hoped, owning her own car had helped Jenny begin to unravel the apron strings.

Ruefully. Meg thought, *now if I could just say the same for myself.*

She counted on having Jenny with her for one more year. Then, as Claire had done, Jenny would go off to college and wouldn't live under her mother's roof again.

Sometimes Meg wished she could turn back the clock and start all over again, when her daughters were babies. Maybe the second time around, she would do a better job of parenting.

One thing was certain. Meg wouldn't have tolerated Jack Kites for half her life, not again. For twenty-five years she'd waited for him to find his own happiness and contentment, a fruitless search that always seemed to be at the expense of his wife and children.

For twenty-five years, a quarter of a century, as a constant refrain punctuating all other aspects of her life, she'd told herself repeatedly *If only he'd...*

If only he'd take his antidepressant medication.

If only he could land a college teaching job.

If only he didn't think he was too good to punch an ordinary time-clock and work for a living.

If only.

No, she wouldn't have tolerated Jack's nonsense, not with what she'd learned from having done so. Nor Warren's, either.

Some women weren't supposed to be shackled to a man, and in recent years Meg had come to believe she was one of that strange breed. In her experience, men were unreliable, selfish, and thoroughly frustrating. She had abandoned the girlish notion that somewhere out there an ideal man waited for Meg Kites. Besides, it was too damned much trouble...

She stirred the meat sauce on the stove and was getting ready to boil the noodles when Jenny brought the cottage cheese and diet soda.

"Mom, I hate to say anything, but your hair is really turning silver."

Her daughter's remark surprised her. "You've noticed. I did, too, this morning. Maybe you could buy a rinse in town."

"What shade?"

"I don't know. Dark brown?"

"You don't want it to look artificial. How about a nice ash-brown? They say as you get older, you need to go lighter. It softens your face."

"Ash-brown, eh? Well, okay. Whatever you think, Jenny. I'm game."

"Or you could just let it go. Let it all turn silver."

"No, not yet. I'll try a rinse first. I mean, when your own daughter comments on your silver hair, it tends to give a woman pause."

"Then I'll get the rinse and I'll help you put it on tomorrow."

"Before or after we talk about the important thing you need to discuss?"

Jenny just smiled, kissed Meg's cheek, and left.

Well, she'd have a jumbo pan of lasagna Jenny wouldn't be home to eat. Meg would have been satisfied with wheat crackers and a bowl of broccoli florets or steamed asparagus. Draining the noodles, she assembled the casserole and slid it into the oven, setting the timer for fifty-five minutes. She gazed around the empty kitchen, at a loss. For some unaccountable reason, she suddenly felt lonely, almost as if she might cry.

What on earth had come over her? Was she saddened because Jenny was growing up, or because in the foreseeable future her youngest child would be gone?

She pulled out the piano bench, opened some sheet music, and pounded out all three movements of a Beethoven sonata. When the timer rang, Meg's mood had changed, and she was no longer suffused with a nameless dread.

She removed the lasagna from the oven, balanced the pan on a trivet on the counter to cool, and walked out to the backyard to check her tomato crop.

With a plastic laundry basket, she went from plant to plant, gently detaching the fragrant Big Girl tomatoes and placing them in the basket. Twelve Roma plants, her Italian paste tomatoes, would survive the first hard frost, when she'd pull them from the vine and spend an afternoon in the kitchen making sauce to store in the basement freezer.

It was just as well that Jenny's car was mobile again, for Meg had disliked those pre-dawn trips to Burger Master. She hadn't been able to forget the image of the tall, pale man, almost believing he'd been trying to communicate something to her. Why else would she have seen him, if he hadn't willed her to?

Which was simply ridiculous, and her saner side knew it. Any car with any driver could have been traveling the road at that particular time and day. It just so happened that Meg Kites was the lucky winner.

Sure, Meg. Similar to winning the lottery, one chance in seven million.

When Meg was a child, her mother had believed her daughter was psychic. Meg's dreams could be so vivid she sometimes woke up screaming. Once she'd dreamed her grandfather was going to die, and the following week a tire had come off a car on the Interstate, bounced into her grandfather's windshield and killed him instantly. After that dream, Meg was taken to see Father Cavanaugh at the Catholic Church, for prayer.

She'd grown up believing there was something wrong with her, something unlike other children. Meg had tried to follow the Father's instructions to *conscientiously objectify* the strange feelings that came to her, to stifle the thoughts and images.

"Trust only in what you can touch and see and learn about with your rational mind, Mary Margaret," the good Father said. "In every-thing but trust and faith in the Lord. Remember, the mind is the Devil's battlefield."

His simple remedy for Meg of a cookie and warm milk before prayers at bedtime were religiously followed by her mother.

But when Meg made a firm resolve not to tamper with what Father Cavanaugh termed things of the occult, her faith had been swept right out the door, as well. And the only person she had truly been able to trust in life was herself. Now she attended a Baptist church, and she hadn't bothered with a novena in years.

Finding a prize Big Boy tomato, Meg thought that if Mister Mortician had been searching for a sensitive, he'd barked up the wrong tree. She refused to have any part in becoming a conduit for his messages.

Odd, when she remembered it now, how she'd never mentioned that peculiar part of her childhood to either of her daughters. Even today, she still felt there was something embarrassing about it. And besides, her kids thought she was goofy enough without believing their own mother was even suspected of being psychic, to boot.

The sun was sinking low in the meadow behind her house. She looked up at the clear sky to spot the evening star, but saw one small, pitch-black cloud, a dense black mass with a greenish tinge around the edges that almost seemed to pulsate.

Meg picked up the basket and headed toward the house, calling in the dogs and cats before shutting the doors and lowering the windows against the sudden night chill.

From time to time, she looked out to see if the ominous cloud formation was still in the sky, only to find the cloud in the same position through dusk, hovering over her backyard.

She had lived in many places, in differing parts of Virginia, in other states, but she had never witnessed the sight of a single storm cloud in an otherwise cloudless sky. Meg didn't know why, but she found it unsettling, and wished Jenny were home. She even willed the cloud to go away.

At ten o'clock as she dressed for bed, Sweet Babu mewed at the door to go outside. When she opened the back door, the cloud was no longer there.

But as she watched the night sky, a brilliant meteor streaked across the heavens. A smile crept to her lips as she made a wish, something she hadn't done since her daughters were children, not for years.

Waiting to let the cat in, Meg realized how dull life really was, with no room for magic and mystery. The shooting star had been a gentle reminder. Well, what could be so wrong with making a wish, even if it were destined to never come true?

She had wished for a small romance to come into her life. She wasn't *that* old. It *could* happen. Couldn't it?

With ash-brown hair and the application of more beauty lotion, the day might come when she pushed a cart down the aisle at the supermarket and collided with a middle-aged Prince Charming.

Yeah, right Meg – like in one of those old movies starring Rock Hudson and Doris Day.

Nonetheless, she climbed into bed that night hoping for a wonderful dream.

****

On Sunday morning Meg took her coffee to sit on the back porch. The first thing catching her eye was the row of drooping tomato plants, their leaves shimmering in the early-morning sunlight. Setting her cup on the porch railing, she ventured down the steps to the yard to take a closer look.

A clear, jelly-like substance had covered the tomatoes and coated patches of the lawn. The cats sniffed, fastidiously lifting their paws to avoid stepping in it.

Meg touched the jelly that felt like cold glue on her fingers. With a large spoon, she scooped some of it into a plastic container, snapped on a lid, and placed it in the refrigerator. Now she would have two oddities for Theodore Rucker, the County Agricultural Extension Agent. If anyone could find out what this stuff was, Ted had to be the man.

As the sun rose higher in the sky, the substance seemed to melt. With dismay, she saw that the vines of her tomato plants had withered and died. She had just enough Romas to make a medium-sized batch of her famous 1940's Victory Garden Chili Sauce.

In the afternoon she occupied herself at the kitchen stove wielding a wooden spoon over a large enamelware kettle filled with vinegar, peeled and crushed tomatoes, chopped bell peppers and onions, brown sugar, nutmeg and ginger and other spices. A mélange of ingredients to cook over low heat for ten hours: Meg planned to take several jars to her best friend Chris Phlegar when she went to a conference in Richmond in early November. She and Chris had an unspoken agreement: Meg's sauce in exchange for quarts of sweet figs Chris's mother marked Fragile and sent by UPS from Pensacola, Florida.

Before dinner, Jenny called to say she wouldn't be home until Monday. She and Nell and Brianna were driving into town to see a movie and planned to stay at Brianna's overnight.

Tossing an olive branch, Jenny said, "But I bought the rinse. We can do it Monday night."

"Okay. Have a good time and be careful driving after dark."

"You're not mad, are you?"

"Goodness, no. Why would I be mad? I can't wait to go into work Monday morning looking like a silver fox."

"Mom!"

"Just kidding. Love you."

"Love you, too."

With the cats at her feet and Cherry Lamb snuffling in her sleep over a furnace vent, Meg spent the evening in front of a made-for-TV movie, writing a long, newsy letter to Claire sprinkled with amusing anecdotes about Jenny on-the-job.

In the morning, she awoke to a hard frost. She packed the ubiquitous carton of yogurt, a banana, celery and carrot strips, and a package of reduced-fat microwave popcorn for lunch. In a separate bag she placed the jar of Clorox and water.

When she reached into the refrigerator for the plastic container and lifted the lid, the jelly-like substance she'd spooned into the container Sunday morning had disappeared. But she'd take it in, anyway. Maybe Ted could find some sort of residue to analyze.

There had to be a rational explanation for it, Meg was convinced.

Chapter Four

"Mr. Feder! If it's not too much of an imposition, may I ask what you're doing?"

Thinking she was the first to arrive, Meg had unlocked the outer doors of the County Department of Social Services twenty minutes early, only to find Norm Feder sitting at her desk behind the closed door, riffling through a sheaf of papers in her Out-box.

At once, the short wisp of a man predictably wearing one of his two threadbare polyester leisure suits – this one faded salmon, the other pea-green – leaped up from Meg's chair. She was amazed to see a look of embarrassment on his ferret-like face, a reality that under the circumstances almost made him seem human.

"I was only wondering if you had work for me to do, Meg, as I'd been gone for a few days on medical leave. I...uh...well, I arrived early, as you can see, with every intention of starting the week with a bang, a little jump-start, as it were."

As it were? Who talked like that, with the single exception of Mr. Feder? She'd have called him Norm, but he had pointedly requested she address him only by his surname. As his supervisor, surely Meg was too lowly to use his hallowed Christian name.

Oh, Lord, but she felt too weary to deal with this.

"Mr. Feder, please push the door shut and have a seat."

He did as she asked, his face now a mask of guileless innocence.

"Why, what's on your mind, Meg?"

"You. You're on my mind, far too much and much too often." She collapsed into her chair with a sigh. "I'd like to request that you consider a transfer out of this department. If you would be so kind."

He rubbed his hands together with a strange enthusiasm and

tapped his foot. "I should say not! I enjoy my work. I wouldn't dream of asking for a transfer."

With a look of defiance in his beady brown eyes, he folded his arms across his bird-like chest, daring her to make the next move in their insane little chess game that had intensified over the long, interminable span of fifteen years.

She could see how he relished her discomfort, wondering how the tables had turned when he was the party obviously in the wrong. She smoothed her hand over her forehead and took a deep breath.

"It's become painfully apparent to me, over the years, how you heartily resent my supervision. Would you mind telling me why?"

"Why would you think that? Have I done anything untoward to indicate I resent you? Oh, surely not!"

"On a daily basis. Or weren't you aware of it?" Her tone had slipped over the line into pure sarcasm, but she was beyond caring. "I've often wondered if it isn't because I was hired by the welfare board for the director's position, when you had submitted your application due to your belief you had seniority in the department and were the one person to be a shoe-in for the job."

"All in your mind, Meg, my dear. Perhaps you need to have your head examined." His rodent-like eyes glittered.

"Come on, Norm. Let's be blunt. You're making my life exceedingly unpleasant. People continually complain about your superior, unhelpful attitude. I've arrived at the conclusion this agency would be better served if you weren't around."

"You can't get rid of me, oh, no! I'm a Merit System employee, a career bureaucrat. I opted long ago for job security and a hefty retirement. I have no intention of going anywhere. Wild horses couldn't drag me away, as it were, heh-heh."

Now his long, thin fingers made a steeple beneath his chin, as Mr. Feder clearly believed himself to be in the driver's seat.

Recklessly, Meg charged ahead. "There's also the problem of your attitude with our clients. They come to us for public assistance because they're down on their luck. It's humiliating enough, without you behaving as if it's all their fault and they should be ashamed to have the audacity to ask for help."

"Well, excuse me for having a Puritan work ethic! Our clients are wastrels, if you want my honest opinion. But be that as it may, my paperwork is flawless, and I defy you to find fault with it."

Be that as it may? She could feel herself losing it as she focused on Mr. Feder sitting in the chair beside her desk like an evil goblin, seeming to grow inches a minute before her incredulous eyes, an indomitable presence dumped into her life to make the twilight years of her career in social services a living hell.

"A *monkey* could fill out those forms! *Surely* you don't feel as if you're making some unique contribution with your damned *paperwork*!"

She had tiptoed to the edge of supervisory boundaries, and then she'd plowed right over them, and from the way she felt at the moment, the Devil could take the hindmost because she just didn't care.

The Devil could take the hindmost? Where had *that* come from? One of Mr. Feder's expressions, no doubt.

Mr. Feder's pencil-mark lips worked for several seconds before he managed to spew out his words. "If you ask me, *your* superiors could find some room for improvement in the job you do. I'm hardly the worthless monkey you take me for. I have eyes." He thumped his scrawny chest. "Don't think I haven't seen what goes on around here, your preferential treatment of certain employees, a case in point passing over a seasoned veteran such as myself for plum promotions time and time again. And don't believe for a single moment I haven't documented every infraction, too! Why, I'll be more than willing to testify about what I know in a court of law! No one would need to subpoena Norman Feder to appear before the bench. No, indeed!"

Oh, this ought to be rich. Meg took another deep breath and sat back in her chair. Poor Mr. Feder. What a miserable excuse for a human being he was.

"Norm, when hell freezes over and you have the opportunity to do my performance evaluation, you'll get the chance to fry my ass. But until that time comes, and don't hold your breath, I get to fry yours. Which is precisely what I shall do, if I ever find you in my office again, going through my papers. Do you understand?"

His voice was deadly-soft. "Are we finished here?"

"Not quite. Do you understand?"

"Oh, yes. Perfectly."

"Good. Then you're excused."

"Dismiss me as if I were a mere schoolboy? Oh, you'll rue this day, I can assure you!"

She watched as he opened the door and flounced from the office with exaggerated dignity. She knew too much about his personal life, which didn't make it easier to dislike him as vehemently as she did.

Norm Feder lived alone in a boarding house, drove a Pontiac older than Meg's car, and squirreled away every dime he earned, God only knew for what. He was forty-six years of age, had a Masters in Social Work, had never been married, and was not gay. What a shame, for he was truly asexual, the most sexless man Meg had ever encountered.

He didn't own a pet, not even a goldfish.

He was so stingy that he never contributed to office pools to buy flowers when someone's husband died, and forget going-away gifts for departing staff.

He had never been to lunch with a coworker, not once that anyone knew about, not in twenty years. In fact, like Meg, he brought his lunch to work and ate at his desk.

He was the first one in the office, and the last to leave. And he was right; he would sit here earning a salary while exercising no creativity, originality, or initiative until he retired. And delight in driving Meg Kites to the brink of insanity in the process.

Dear God! No wonder the taxpayers beefed about the government getting too big for its britches! Without this job, Norm Feder would be in the food stamps line, Puritan work ethic be damned. No one with half a brain would hire him. He was a...*a drip*!

Well, the battle lines had been drawn. Norm knew where Meg stood, and vice versa. But she'd have been willing to wager he'd never again come snooping around in her office.

How long had *that* been going on? At least now she knew how the rumors about the contents of confidential memos had been circulated around the office.

The little twerp!

The intercom buzzed, interrupting her demented reverie.

"Mrs. Kites, it's the County Manager. Urgent. Line twelve."

"Thanks, Joanne," she said to the receptionist, then punched into the right line and waited for today's dose of let's-give-Meg-Kites-hell.

"Hey, Meg? One of the Supervisors got a citizen complaint on Saturday about well-heeled welfare recipients using food stamps to buy frozen Alaskan king crab legs in the supermarket and driving away in a vintage Dodge Viper. Don't you and your people tell those sons of bitches to eat beans and cornbread?"

Once again, the day seemed endless, but at last Meg pulled into the driveway of her own house. Only to find Jenny bawling at the kitchen table.

"Mom, I just read this vicious letter from Dad! I can't do anything right! You know how hard I've been working at Burger Master. *He* seemed to think I'm fooling around. That's a direct quote: fooling around. Here. Read this."

Meg skimmed the letter in Jack's familiar, disjointed hand, the oversized childlike letters sprawled across the page.

"I have to say I don't know why you're this upset, Jenny. He only reminded you about college. Nothing wrong with that."

"Yeah, and he also wants to know what I'm doing with the money I earn."

"Well, what do you know? Having wondered the same thing a time or two myself, I'd be interested in hearing, as well."

Jenny's face changed, growing cloudy as she went on the defensive. "I'm saving it! I told you!"

"For what?"

"That's what I wanted to talk with you about. Nell and Brianna and I plan to move into a trailer. It's really nice, only three-fifty a month. Electric heat, three bedrooms, two baths, modern appliances."

Meg felt herself stiffen into the Mean-Mom Mode. "Out of the question. You have a home here."

"But I need to be on my own! I'm eighteen. I can do what I want now."

"Oh, Jenny," Meg said wearily. "Is that a threat?"

"I'd like your approval." But she didn't need Meg's approval. Though Jenny didn't say it, the inference was there.

Meg got up from the table, shrugged off her blazer and hung it over the back of a chair. She went to the kitchen sink and looked out the window, trying to weigh her words, praying she wouldn't say the wrong thing.

She turned around to face her daughter.

"What I'd like to ask is, if you're not going to be with me, why did I spend my last dime on this house?"

"The trailer's only a few miles away, Mom. I'll be over all the time. There's no washer and dryer there, and I'll have to do my uniforms."

"Jenny, it's not the same and you know it. Try and understand my point of view. I thought you'd be with me until you leave for college next fall."

"Now I don't know if I want to."

"College? When did this pop into your head? No, never mind, don't tell me. I think you need to call your father and discuss it with him. All of it. I'm just tired, Jenny. You'll have to forgive me and let me off the hook, for once."

"You *know* I can't talk to Dad. I need you on my side!"

"And I need time to think it through. You can't spring this on me and expect me to be ecstatic."

After a brief silence, Jenny said, "No, I suppose not. But you can't live through me, Mom. You should have your own life."

And what could Meg say to that? Jenny was right on the mark.

"At least when Claire moved out, she went off to college. You know you can't stay at Burger Master forever."

"Claire's the favorite child," Jenny said sourly. "She always has been, and she always will be."

How could a daughter she so loved try and push her so far away? They were getting nowhere fast, and Meg decided it would be best to change the subject.

"By the way, did you remember to bring my rinse?"

"It's in the bathroom. You want me to help?"

"I think I can manage." She glanced at Jenny and smiled. "If I'm going to be living alone, I'd best learn to do for myself."

Visibly, Jenny exhaled a sigh of relief. "Well, I have to run, Mom. Nell and I are going to sign the lease on the trailer tonight. We can move in the middle of October."

"That's two weeks away!"

"But I can pack this weekend. Brianna's boyfriend Joe said we could move things in his truck. It'll all work out, Mom. Honest."

"Okay, sweetheart. I hope so. But if the bottom falls out, at least you still have your room here. I promise not to rent it to some cute middle-aged hunk."

"Oh, please!"

"And you have to call your Dad. Tonight, and no excuses. If you're at Brianna's or Nell's, call collect."

"I will. But don't wait up for me. I'll be home late. Tomorrow I work the one-to-nine shift."

After Jenny had flown the coop, Meg drew a hot bath, stripped off her clothes, and sank into water up to her neck. With her eyes closed and thoughts colliding in her brain, she stayed in the bathtub until the water cooled. Then she got out, read the instructions on the box of hair rinse, leaned over the tub, and gave it a whirl.

An hour later she used the blow-dryer, anxious to see how she looked as an ash-brown. Not so hot, but the silver had taken on reddish highlights. She wouldn't really be able to tell until morning, in natural light. And if it looked like hell, so what? She could always dye it dark brown again.

Or maybe patent-leather black and paint her eyebrows black and wear flame-red lipstick, chase around the house with a coat-hanger and behave toward her daughters like Joan Crawford as Mommy Dearest.

For the one bright note of the day, Ted Rucker had called her office at three-thirty that afternoon, anxious to let her know the results of lab work on her samples.

"A very mild bleach and water solution," Ted said.

"I know that, Ted! I mixed it myself. What I wanted to know

was, why did it come to a boil sitting in a plastic bucket on my basement steps?"

"I've done a lot of thinking on the topic. I even talked to a physics professor."

"Well, you didn't need to go that far." Although momentarily she was glad he had, with so little else in her life to claim a flicker of excitement.

"Friendly Cooperative Extension, at your service. Besides, I was curious. It's not a chemical reaction. So, we got to yammering about electromagnetic fields, fault lines in the earth's crust, tectonic plates and all that jazz. Are you with me on this?"

"You're telling me I had a little earthquake?"

"Not exactly. All kinds of weird junk happens in the natural world. There's Meaden's plasma vortex theory, which has to do with electrically charged air currents. You've heard of those mysterious circles in Britain's wheat fields, some as much as eighty feet across. They all seem to occur within thirty miles of Stonehenge, the Druids' ancient shrine.   Some think UFOs come down from the sky to make the circles, but Meaden chalks it off as air currents generated by powerful electromagnetic currents associated with Stonehenge. The ancients had some instinctive way of knowing where to build their sacred places, apparently."

Meg had visualized Ted at the other end of the phone, cowboy boots propped on his desk, faded jeans, and a plaid flannel shirt. His real job was dealing with local farmers, and he was always ready to take a few minutes to hunker.

"Okay. What about the plastic container? Did you find anything?"

"You said the stuff on your tomatoes looked like clear sticky jelly, right? Well, we found some ammonia and a little phosphorus. But Dr. Yerling wanted to know something else. Did you happen to see anything unusual in the atmosphere prior to the jelly episode?"

"Saturday, late in the day and on toward dusk, there was this one deep-black cloud with shimmering edges. Oh, and later on a shooting star. I don't know how unusual it is, or whether I'm not as observant ordinarily as some people might be."

"Man, I wish I'd been there! Yerling called it star-jelly, often associated with an ultra-bright meteor. And he called it something else, too. Thought you might be interested."

He let the silence deepen. Ted had decided to deliberately toy with her.

She took the bait. "Quit it. Of course I'm interested. Tell me."

"Skyfall. You may have heard of strange skyfalls. Schools of fish dumped in the middle of the desert, toads, ten-penny nails."

"Skyfall. How interesting."

"Chances are one multiplied by infinity squared you'll ever have an experience like that again, Meg. Yerling asked me to ask you whether you've had any strange dream activity lately."

"Not that I can remember. Why?"

"He says your house out in Wilson County may be sitting on something similar to ley lines. Spelled l-e-y, Old English for meadow. A super energy point."

"You're making me have spooky feelings, Ted. Stop it."

He treated himself to a self-indulgent chuckle but, after all, he'd earned it. "Hey, Meg. Channelers search a lifetime for places on an energy point. Maybe you should contemplate hanging out a shingle and become a palm reader."

Palm reader: a memory tugged at the edge of her mind, but she couldn't quite reach it.

"Thanks for the help, Ted. You told me more than I wanted to know."

Skyfall: a presage of what? Was it something that had happened out of the blue? Or had it occurred because Meg Kites attracted it? She didn't want to entertain such an idea, yet she couldn't push it from her thoughts. The old *Twilight Zone* theme played in her head.

She broke down and made a bowl of instant tapioca pudding and ate it with a cup of decaf coffee while watching *Jeopardy!* She found herself weighing the pros and cons of Jenny's plan to live on her own in a trailer, but as she reminded herself, isn't that what a mother is supposed to do?

Pros: Jenny would learn to manage her money, or not. She would become more independent and responsible. She'd find out the difficulties involved in living with other people, even two good friends.

Cons? Jack would have a royal fit. Jenny might decide to put off college indefinitely. And she wouldn't be under Meg's roof, hence subject to her daily scrutiny.

And Meg suspected the last item on the Cons list was the real reason Jenny wanted to move out.

In truth, Jenny had cut the umbilical cord years ago, the very year Jack left, when her friends had become the center of her life. Meg had been virtually alone with the animals for a year, before she'd met and fallen in love with Warren.

In retrospect, she realized how Warren had been as controlling as Jack had been, maybe more so. After he died, she wondered how she could have duped herself into believing he really cared for her. If he had cared enough, perhaps he'd have done something about his drinking. But Warren had always done things his way, living exactly as he'd wished to live with apologies to no one, and he'd even died by choice. Meg's feelings were the least of his concerns.

If her enabling personality predisposed her to find Jacks and Warrens, Meg knew she really would be better off by herself. Sometimes she wished she'd gone into any field other than social work. Being society's official caretaker had contaminated her personal life.

In what other line of work could a professional be subject to such vilification, not to mention staff members like Norman Feder? She was aware that Marty Flynn, the County Manager, viewed her operation as a sick joke.

"How about funding the fraud investigator position I put in the budget request?" she'd said to Marty, as a response to his irate phone call about the frozen crab legs. "Then we could put a staff member on the road in an unmarked county vehicle, to drive by all the client houses and look for Dodge Vipers parked in driveways."

A lightbulb went off in her brain. Norm Feder, Fraud Investigator. Thank you, God!

Get the troublemaker out of the office, make him feel important, give him unlimited use of a county car, let him appear in Court to testify against the *wastrels*. How he would enjoy himself!

She'd think it through, clear it with Marty, pitch it to Mr. Feder tomorrow, and reassign the man whose secret office moniker was The Slimeball to begin a week from today.

Her opening gambit would be, "Remember how you told me about your strong Puritan work ethic?"

He could be the Clint Eastwood of the supermarket check-out lines, monitoring the purchases made by food stamp recipients, slithering out to the parking lot to inventory what models of cars they drove. Perfect!

Meg finally had a clear image of the creature Mr. Feder most reminded her of: a black widow spider.

Having decided to re-read *Madame Bovary*, Meg called in the cats and went to bed early. One thing about living alone: she could do what she wanted when she wanted. Tonight, she felt like weeping for Emma's poor husband because he loved her so much and was deemed such a loathsome being. Too simple and predictable to suit reckless Emma.

She had become thoroughly absorbed in Flaubert when Bart leaped like a freight train on her chest. His hair stood on end. His green saucer eyes fixed on her. He hissed and dug his fishhook claws into her stomach.

Meg shoved him to the end of the bed. "What's your problem? Be good!"

Then Cappy started hissing in the middle of the room, frightening Babu and making him flee for shelter beneath the bed.

And Cherry Lamp yelped nonstop, until Meg climbed from the warm confines of bed to let her outside.

She remained in the kitchen and drank a glass of skim milk, waiting for the dog to scratch at the door to get in. Then she brushed her teeth, turned out the lights, and felt her way into the dark bedroom.

Finding the edge of the bed, Meg glanced out the window overlooking the backyard.

On a clear, moonless autumn night, in an upstairs window of the old log house, she saw a light burning.

In the year 1891, after extensive scientific inquiry and at considerable expense, he awaited railway delivery of the cabinet from the Ralph E. Silvestre Company in Chicago.

It was dark polished wood, eight feet tall by four feet in width, with a depth of two and one-half feet. Brass-hinged double doors and brass corner plates made the cabinet of such handsome quality as to warrant an honored display in the finest parlor of the day, yet such was not its purpose.

The final requirement was for modest but finely calibrated modifications of his own design.

He had entered the dark enclosure, shutting the doors behind him, a procedure he had executed fifty times or more. He could hear her voice outside, the only sound in a vast, hushed silence.

Though he could not see her, he knew that she turned the giant hourglass displayed conspicuously center-stage.

At an appointed time, the doors were to open to a darkness where once he had stood.

Her instructions were to turn the cabinet on its casters around and around. When she opened the doors a second time, there he would be, seemingly drained, exhausted by his inexplicable ordeal.

Reaching for his hand, with some apparent difficulty she would lead him from the cabinet and into the light...

...to a thunderous standing ovation.

Chapter Five

October twentieth brought an abrupt change of season from Virginia's extended Indian summer into fall. A cold wind spewed rain from the east, ripping the last leaves from the trees.

At dusk, Meg carried out the garbage to the shed at the far corner of her one-third acre. A steady drizzle fell, promising another hard frost when temperatures were predicted to dip into the low twenties well before midnight.

Already, she sensed the icy snap in the air and wondered whether the rain would turn to snow. She had not thought to wear a sweater over her T-shirt, and by the time she finished transferring the wastebasket trash into a larger garbage pail, she was chilled to the bone.

A mournful wind gusting through the pines and over the meadow made her feel desolate and isolated, yet she was only a few yards from her own back door. A steely rain pelted her face and arms. On second thought, sleet seemed more likely than snow flurries.

Each night she had looked for the light in the log house but hadn't witnessed its mysterious glow in the upstairs window a second time. Perhaps it had been an optical illusion, a light from another source reflected off the glass windowpane.

Starting across the lawn to her door, she happened to glance at the old house.

A diaphanous white shape hovered on the front porch. Somehow it gave an impression of timid reticence, as if it didn't want to be seen. The figure of a woman?

But the image was so blurred by the driving rain that Meg doubted her perception. The sound of her own voice seemed startling when she called out, "Hello?"

She walked to the back fence for a better view, watching her footing around an arrangement of small flowering plants she'd set out to bloom in spring. But when she looked again, the vision was gone.

If in fact it had ever been there. She felt like a nearsighted fool.

Probably a patch of fog trapped in the mist, dissipated by the wind. Quickly, she jogged to her house and locked the doors.

Most of the hours at home for the next few days were consumed by helping Jenny decide what to pack for the move. On Saturday Joe, the taciturn and sullen boyfriend, appeared with a pick-up truck. Meg was stymied by how a girl as attractive and upbeat as Brianna could be attracted to such a boy.

She helped Jenny and her friends carry boxes out to the truck, the fragile items such as dishes and Jenny's snow-globe collection packed in the hatch of Meg's car. She followed them to the community of Minter Springs on the far side of Wilson County, the sole parent whose presence marked the event.

She was shocked as the three vehicles drove up to the trailer sitting like a huge luxury liner on a back road several miles in from the main highway to town. She might have guessed: Jenny's low-slung Mazda would never be able to traverse this stretch of road after a snowfall or ice storm.

But she'd have bitten off her tongue before uttering a negative word, for Jenny and her girlfriends sailed on a wave of happiness.

"What do you think of it, Mom?"

"I think I should live here, and you kids can have my house. This wasn't what I had in mind when you mentioned a trailer." She handed a box to Joe, who took it from her grudgingly.

Terrific, Meg thought to herself. Joe would evolve into yet another country man wearing a baseball cap destined to drive around all day in his pick-up truck claiming he was self-employed, while his wife slaved in a garment factory doing piecework at a sewing machine for minimum wage ten hours a day, six days a week, to support him and their children.

"Look inside!" Jenny actually pulled Meg by the hand. "It's a mess yet. We'll need time to arrange things."

Meg received the guided tour. Brianna's boxes were stacked in one bedroom, Nell's in another.

"Have your parents seen this?" Meg asked in general.

Nell laughed. "Yeah, my Dad did. He says he can't wait to see what our first electric bill is, when we turn on the heat."

"You know, this really makes me wish I'd looked into buying the old house in back of mine," Meg said, articulating a thought that had lingered half-formed in her mind. "Then you could have lived there, and you wouldn't have been so far off the main road, and you wouldn't have had to worry about rent, either."

"Mom, that old house hasn't been lived in for years," Jenny said. "It doesn't even have indoor plumbing. Thanks a bunch. What could we do, share the outhouse with the red squirrel?"

"But if I were to buy it, I could put in a bathroom, then a small furnace..."

"Forget it, Mom. It's probably a wreck inside, anyway."

"You never know. Maybe not."

"But look how nice our bathrooms are!"

Meg had to admit the living arrangements in the opulent trailer had real possibilities. And with electric heat, at least they wouldn't freeze to death, even if the bill was so outrageous Jenny ended up having to ask her mother's help to pay it.

But when that unaccountably lonely feeling threatened to engulf her, she turned to Jenny. "Give me a hand unloading the car. I need to be home before dark."

With everything Jenny owned neatly stacked in the third bedroom, Meg felt like a fifth wheel and made her excuses to leave. She pressed a twenty-dollar bill into Jenny's hand, then added a ten. Kissing her on the cheek, Meg told her to take her friends out for pizza, to celebrate.

"I'll call you!" Jenny waved her mother down the driveway.

Meg clocked the distance from the trailer to her house, twenty-two miles, in a direction diametrically opposite from the route she took to go to her office, which certainly precluded frequent stopped-by-to-say-Hi visits.

The end of October wasn't for another eight days, and already Jenny had moved out.

Chapter Six

Unfortunately, the County Manager was unable to make a unilateral decision to approve Meg's request to reconfigure an existing staff position. Instead, the proposal had to be included as an agenda item for an in-depth discussion during the Executive Session of the Board of Supervisors' Monday night meeting. And when you put it before the Board, seven officials whose primary goal was to be re-elected, anything could happen, and might. Democracy in action, Marty quipped.

At Marty's suggestion, Meg had garnered supporting documentation from other local welfare departments around the Commonwealth. Reams of proof were provided, that employing a welfare fraud investigator served a dual, politically correct purpose, not only returning fraudulently obtained revenues to the General Fund but enabling vigorous prosecution of evil, fork-tongued malingerers.

Meg had little choice but to heed Marty's sardonic advice to hurry up and wait, and exercise even more patience while the decision-making wheels of the bureaucracy creaked in their rusty cogs.

Finally, the day she prayed for arrived, when Marty telephoned to say the reclassification had been unanimously approved by the Board.

She called Norman Feder into her office on a Friday afternoon to make the pitch she had rehearsed countless times, confident she'd given it just the right, irresistible spin.

"Not interested," came his infuriating response.

"But why? This is a promotion."

"Not to me, it isn't. I don't like to drive any more than is absolutely necessary. I dislike driving to such an extent that, were my rooming house not so far away, I'd walk to work."

"Mr. Feder, I don't think you have a choice in this matter. Each of us has to be flexible and accept new job responsibilities as assigned."

"I have every choice. I can choose to refuse the assignment, and I do. And you know as well as I, there's not a thing you can do about it. Not with *my* seniority."

In the face of the man's prissy obstinance, Meg felt more than willing to throw in the towel. It had been a long week with crucial deadlines to meet. Since noon, with plans of a sort for the weekend, she'd been counting the minutes until five o'clock.

When she witnessed Mr. Feder's readiness to engage in a mental fencing match, Meg knew it was one fringe benefit she could rightfully deny him. The man was a hopeless case, and nothing she could say would make him budge from his two-windowed office with the brass nameplate on the door.

Besides, why beat a dead horse? She rose from her desk chair and began to gather her things.

"You're right. When the County Manager asked me for one good man, one individual absolutely trustworthy and with long tenure in the department, someone so seasoned that he knows the welfare regs like the back of his hand, I naturally thought of Norman Feder. But now I can see my judgment was a bit flawed. So sorry to have troubled you, Mr. Feder."

"The...uh...the County Manager?"

"Oh, did I forget to mention Marty? I apologize once again. Just tired, I guess. It's been quite a week, what with all the demands from the state office. Now, if you'll excuse me, I plan to make a beeline for my car and hustle home."

"Meg, I'm only asking for a moment of your valuable time and a bit of clarification. Surely you can spare so little for a senior staff member such as myself."

In a light tone of voice, she said, "You're not going to make my day and turn in your letter of resignation, are you?"

"Please, sit, sit, sit for a minute!" He actually fluttered his hands.

"Okay," she said, taking her seat. "What's on your mind?"

"The County Manager. You were going to say?"

She put her elbows on the desk and paused as if pondering grave issues. "It's a bit complicated to explain, since this is the first time for such an arrangement. But the fraud investigator will be a liaison between the local Welfare Board and the Board of Supervisors. Dually supervised by myself and Marty."

Which was a damned lie. But Meg knew how tempting such a proposition would be to Mr. Feder, his golden opportunity to stab her in the back with any excuse, real or imagined, second only to seeing her body flattened by a Greyhound bus.

Eagerly, Mr. Feder said, "And Martin Flynn asked for me, specifically?"

What a dreamer.

"Actually, your name was mentioned by Marty even before I had an opportunity to blurt it out. Your long and illustrious service has not been overlooked by those in the seat of power, I can assure you."

He was almost breathless when he said, "Why, I'm flattered!"

"Oh, Norm, don't give me that. You've earned this attention, and you know it better than anyone."

His nut-brown eyes sparkled behind his ancient wire-rimmed spectacles. He smacked his lips, crossed his legs, sat back in his chair, making himself comfortable. "Meg, what would I be expected to do, precisely?"

"You mean apart from a lot of driving?"

He fanned his fingers rapidly back and forth, as if to say pooh-pooh. "Don't worry about the driving. What else?"

For a solid minute she folded her hands beneath her chin as if contemplating additional cosmic matters. "Much of that would be up to the investigator himself. The position calls for an intelligent, inventive individual willing to carve out his own piece of pie, define the parameters of the job and let Marty and me know how it's to be structured. Probably one of the most autonomous positions within county personnel. Marty would have the ultimate review and approval, of course. And if the job is done well, there's no telling where it could lead somewhere down the pike. Executive Assistant to the County Manager was one thing mentioned."

The luster in his eyes diminished as he sized her up carefully. "All right. What's the catch, Meg? This sounds too good to be true. And I can't help but wonder why you'd suddenly throw a bone my way."

Again, she rose from her chair, picked up her briefcase and hand-bag. There seemed to be no alternate way to deal with the worm, God help her, other than to exit the premises post haste. "Norm, you old skeptic, you," she said as she removed the car keys from her handbag. "I need a yes or no, because two other people have heard about this new job opportunity through the grapevine, try as we might to keep it all confidential, and they're waiting in line."

His scrawny chest puffed up like a bantam rooster. "When shall I begin?"

"Think about it over the weekend and have a rough outline of how you plan to proceed on my desk Monday morning. Time is of the essence on this one. I'll do anything in my power to expedite this with Marty, believe me. And I have every confidence about the County Manager's position. Who else but Norman Feder could bring his special touch to the new role of fraud investigator?"

"Do I get to go to Court and nail 'em?"

"Not only that, but you'll have full use of an unmarked county vehicle. I'll make sure you'll be able to drive it twenty-four/seven, even on weekends. Gas and oil, of course, are free from the tanks at the country garage."

Mr. Feder's eyes were gleaming as he shook Meg's hand.

Not surprisingly, his thin, bony appendage was cold and clammy.

Chapter Seven

The historical marker on the lawn of the Wilson County Court-house related sketchy details of an obscure, long-forgotten Civil War skirmish that had occurred in Wilson.

Having lived in the South for years as a transplant from Chicago, Meg had developed her own theory as to why the rag-tag Confederates were forced to capitulate in humiliating defeat to the Union Army. The ancestors of the men who claimed to be self-employed were dragged off the farms, given inferior weapons with scant training, and told to fight for the land and the honor of their womenfolk. Given her observations of today's male in the rural South, she supposed such a noble cause just hadn't been motivation enough to win the war.

She also felt that the worst thing to happen in her lifetime was when they ended the military draft. Women worked for a living, maintained a home, and still had babies, and men drove around in pick-up trucks wearing baseball caps, except during NASCAR season, of course, when they sat in front of big-screen televisions drinking Budweiser. Too bad someone didn't pay them for being such die-hard NASCAR fans.

Once she'd been tempted to buy a coffee mug from a gift shop inscribed with the saying, "There are three types of men. Intelligent, rich, and the ones I meet."

On Saturday, people came to town to do their banking and buy groceries, so the parking lot behind the courthouse was packed. The out-of-state license plates had thinned out, now that the season for brilliant fall foliage on the Blue Ridge Parkway bringing flocks of tourists to Wilson had passed.

Meg circled the block and parked in a diagonal space in front of the courthouse. Wilson County's population was just under ten thousand, and she marveled at the throngs of people milling around on Saturday morning. Even the old people were out, greeting friends for a social occasion.

She climbed the steps and went into the Clerk of the Court's office. A woman about Meg's age dressed in a hot-pink polyester skirt with elastic waistband and a white blouse with a limp floppy bow at the neck came to the counter.

"Good morning," Meg said. "I recently bought a house on 862, and I'm interested in seeing who owns the property adjacent to mine. It's an old log house on I don't know how many acres of pastureland."

"I'm sorry, but you'll have to check with the Treasurer's office to see how the taxes are paid to find out who owns it."

"Thanks. I'll be back."

She hurried upstairs to the second floor. An officious woman cast from the same mold as the woman in the Clerk's office manned the counter. Meg related the same request.

"I'll have to pull the tax records. Can you show me on this map where the house and land are located?"

Meg found her house. "This is mine. And the parcel bordering it. I'd like to know who the owner is."

The woman removed a thick file folder from a cabinet. "That's the Hill property. The owner is Melody Hill Branscombe. But the taxes are paid by...let me see here. Taxes are paid by Erin Kelly Sumptner from a bank account in Richmond."

"Do you have an address on Branscombe?"

"Mrs. Branscombe lives in the nursing home."

"You mean in Wilson?"

The woman nodded. "Somerset Manor. Sumptner must be a guardian, or a distant relative. But these records show payment by Sumptner for a number of years back, through a custodial account, I believe."

"So whom would you suggest I contact about the property?"

"I'd begin with Branscombe if I were you."

Meg thanked the woman for her assistance and returned to the Clerk's office. "Here I am again," she said with a smile. "Could you find a deed on this property?" She related the information acquired from the Treasurer's office.

"The Hill property? Oh, I can tell you that without looking it up. It's in a trust for the descendants of the Hill family. Quite a parcel, too."

"I was toying with the idea of buying the old house."

"Well, I don't know that you can, seeing as how it's in a trust. Usually it means it's not for sale at any price."

"What does that mean, exactly?"

"If it's in a trust, the property stays in the family forever. Unless somebody finally decides to sell."

"In perpetuity."

"I think I've heard that term."

"I suppose it wouldn't hurt to contact Mrs. Branscombe and ask about it, anyway."

The woman shrugged and turned on her heel, anxious to return the file to its proper place. The wall clock said eleven-fifty, and on Saturday the county offices closed at noon.

Meg drove home and called Somerset Manor to inquire whether Melody Branscombe was still a resident and to ask about visiting hours on Sunday.

Wondering about her impulsive decision, she stared through her bedroom window at the log house. Nothing untoward had occurred lately...

Oh, dear Lord! *Untoward.*

Would she never be free of Norman Feder?

Chapter Eight

When she returned from the Wilson County courthouse, the remainder of her precious Saturday flew by as Meg chipped away at a list of chores she'd procrastinated about for too long. And though her hours at home were more than accounted for, her thoughts kept circling back to the one topic planted firmly at the front of her brain.

If she could just get inside the old log house and take a look around, she'd quickly determine whether her idea was even feasible, or merely another middle-aged pipedream.

Really, she didn't relish the prospect of major renovation, not with Jenny's college costs somewhere on the horizon, nor could she afford both expenses simultaneously.

Early Sunday morning Meg had her coffee, fed the cats and dog, and dressed for church. With a sigh, she wondered when Jenny and friends would have a phone installed. One week away from home, and already Meg missed her youngest daughter.

She decided to leave early and stop off at the trailer before church, since it was on the way. But when a child was launching her fledgling way toward independence, a mother needed an excuse to pop in and certainly couldn't arrive empty-handed.

In a grocery sack she packed a dozen eggs, margarine, bacon, a hearty loaf of sprouted-wheat bread purchased from a local natural-foods store, and a jar of instant coffee. Adding a container of her homemade blackberry jam, Meg carried the food and her Bible out to the car.

At nine o'clock on an overcast day, last night's frost still coated the car windows. She scraped off the ice while warming her car, entertaining the thought of inviting Jenny to attend church services with her.

But she knew what Jenny's response was likely to be. Months ago her daughter had adamantly refused to continue with Sunday school because the teacher harped on one threadbare theme, the evils of premarital sex. Jenny said she was tired of hearing about it, and Meg couldn't much blame her.

But the eagerness to drop in for a surprise visit with her maternal care-package was instantly dampened when she approached the trailer.

Joe's truck, still covered with hoarfrost, was parked for all the world to see beside Jenny's Mazda and Nell's Escort. Meg thought she was going to scream.

Pretending calm, she parked in back of the truck and, toting the groceries, knocked at the door. Even at the early hour, rap music blared from within. No, not rap – hip-hop, the newest irritant for any rational parent.

In flannel pajamas, Jenny answered. Her young face looked anything but happy to find her mother standing on the doorstoop.
"Hi, Mom. What a surprise."

"I'll just bet," Meg said, handing the sack to Jenny, and stepped inside. "I brought breakfast. I'm on my way to church. Jenny, can I talk to you for a minute?"

Nell sat on the dilapidated sofa, painting her toenails. "Hi, Mrs. Kites."

"Where's Brianna?" Meg asked.

"Uh, with Joe," Jenny said, her sheepish expression too genuine to be disguised.

"Jenny. Nell. I can't believe you allowed that boy to stay here overnight. What's gotten into you girls?"

"Mom. Joe's living here, too, after his father kicked him out of the house. Rent and utilities will be split four ways," Jenny said reasonably.

"Over my dead body. Your father will hear about this if that boy doesn't leave today."

Jenny looked close to tears. "I wish you'd called first, before showing up like this."

"If you had a telephone, I would have. I'm going to leave now, before I say something I might regret. I want him gone, or you're moving back home. No argument. Understood?"

Meg had the sinking feeling she was talking to Mr. Feder rather than her own daughter.

"I'm working day-shift tomorrow," Jenny said. "Come by the drive-through on your way to work, and I'll see if I can get away for a few minutes so we can have a cup of coffee and talk."

"Thanks anyway, Jenny, but I'm on a tight schedule tomorrow." She turned toward the door. "Besides, there's nothing to talk about. You have two options. Either Joe's out of here, or you are."

As she ventured down the icy steps to her car, from behind the closed door she heard Jenny's voice wailing, "I knew it! Leave it to my mom to find out! *Now* what?"

Fighting back tears of her own, Meg drove to the main road and continued on for the few remaining miles to Blessed Rock Baptist in time for adult Sunday school.

She attended a country church with a membership of less than a hundred. The pastor's remarks gave her spiritual nourishment each time she came, which wasn't nearly often enough. Selfishly, she coveted her weekends, and attending church every Sunday was too much of a hassle, not to mention an inconvenience. Get up, get dressed, drive – when she had to do that five days a week merely to survive.

After the service ended, she went out to her car to return home. It was twelve-thirty, the day half over. But not today. Today she'd be home somewhat later.

Driving into the parking lot of the nursing home, Meg couldn't get Jenny out of her thoughts. She refused to imagine Jack's reaction, were he to find out what was going on. He'd missed Jenny's turbulent teenage years entirely, removed by five hundred miles from the daily sobs and hormonal anguish of adolescence, the dating and inevitable heartbreaks. Meg had prided herself on weathering the storm as a single parent, and now this.

Walking into the main entrance of Somerset Manor, Meg made a mental note to place clandestine calls to the mothers of Nell and Brianna. She had met them both before the girls were old enough to drive, when they'd taken turns coordinating chauffeur duty for school events, band practice, slumber parties, shopping expeditions, and movies at the Mall.

The nurse on duty was an Esther Williams, like the swimmer who starred in the lush movies of the 'Forties, but there the resemblance ended. Nurse Williams was a sturdy two-hundred pounder with a sweet face. On her white uniform she sported a colorful   button: *Grow old along with me, the best is yet to be.*

"Please sign the guest register, and I'll take you to see Miss Melody. She's in the day room with some of her friends, watching television."

Watching television with friends on a Sunday afternoon, well, that didn't seem such a dreary life for an old person in a nursing home.

Meg signed her full name and then followed Nurse Williams down an institutional-green corridor. Though the home was immaculate, a faint smell of urine wafted in the air, making Meg think of concealed ostomy bags.

"Here's our girl!" Gently, Nurse Williams leaned over a shrunken crone of a woman in a wheelchair with a purple afghan draped across her lap. "Miss Melody, you have a visitor today! This is Mary Margaret Kites. Say hello to Mrs. Kites."

Vacant watery eyes centered on Meg.

"Nice to meet you, Melody. I'm Meg." She reached out for the woman's withered hand.

"Who?" The voice thin as crackling cellophane sounded like a death rattle.

For some reason, Meg began to feel like an imposter. Uneasily, she glanced around the room at frail old people wrapped in crocheted afghans bunched in wheelchairs, each seeming more ancient than the next. Though the television set was tuned to a Sunday football game, she wondered whether any of the viewers had the slightest inkling of what the images flickering across the screen could have meant.

Nurse Williams' loving attention was still trained on Melody. "Miss Melody, tell Meg how old you are."

"Old? How old?"

"That's right. Ninety-five!" The nurse gave the old lady a hug. "That's my girl!"

Nurse Williams accompanied her to the main foyer. "Poor dear. Lately she's been calling out for her father, often a sign the end is near.

Last week we lost our Mr. Herman, who'd been talking for a week about hearing the big brass band of the angels coming. I suppose he did."

"How long has she been here?"

"As long as I've worked in the nursing home. I've been with Somerset for seventeen years."

"Does she suffer from senility?"

"Alzheimer's. And if you ask me, it's for the best. Mrs. Branscombe has no children. Everyone has died except for a cousin who sends nice packages at Christmas. Oh, she has her lucid moments, but they're few and far between."

Meg patted the nurse's shoulder. "There must be a special place in Heaven for people in your profession. I couldn't do this work. It's so depressing."

"Oh, they begin to seem like family after a while. Did you have a special reason for dropping by today?"

"Yes. She owns some property I thought I might be interested in buying. But now that I've met her, I can see that..."

"When she took ill, her cousin agreed to be the executor of her estate. She lives in Richmond. I can look in the office and find the name for you."

"Is it Erin Sumptner?"

"The name does sound familiar. Let me check." The nurse disappeared behind a door and came back with a file. "A Mrs. Sumptner in Richmond."

"Could I have her address?"

"We don't have it, I'm afraid. This generally happens when a distant relative is responsible for maintaining custodial care. According to our records, Mrs. Sumptner handles things through a law firm in Richmond. Which isn't surprising, when you consider she might not have known Miss Melody very well even in better days."

Meg had a flash of two pigtailed cousins playing as children, and a monolithic chunk of years turning them into virtual strangers.

"Well, thank you for letting me see her."

"Would you care to stop by again? Any time."

"Do you think it would make a difference to her?"

"Never can tell. It might."

"I don't mean to sound heartless, Nurse Williams, but probably not. But I'll send a basket of fruit for Christmas."

"No fruit. Hard candies. She loves hard candies. She's very fond of butterscotch, especially those nice ones from England."

****

Later in the afternoon, Meg called her best friend Chris in Richmond on the wild chance she might find her at home.

She'd met Chris Phlegar when she, Jack, and Claire had lived in Richmond, while Jack was in graduate school and Meg had worked as a therapist in a treatment center for heroin addicts. Beginning at age six, Claire's best friend was Allison Phlegar, Chris's daughter.

"Hey! How's it hanging?" Good old Chris.

She could picture Chris on the phone in one of her laid-back Annie Hall outfits, hunkering in a chair with her feet propped up, much like Ted Rucker. It brought a smile to her lips.

"I'll be in Richmond for one of my dastardly-dull welfare conferences the third and fourth of November. I have a reservation at the Sheraton. Thought I'd treat you to dinner at the hotel."

"Are you still in that racket? I don't know how you can tolerate your job any longer."

"Actually, I can't. Wait till I tell you the newest tale starring Mr. Feder."

"Oh, God! Is that little weasel still around? You haven't thought of a way to can his ass?"

"No, but maybe the next best thing."

"Displayed in stocks on the courthouse green? Shot at sunrise?"

Meg laughed. "Not quite. Could you do me a favor?"

"What?"

"Look in the Richmond phone book and see if there's a listing for an Erin Sumptner."

The sound of pages flipping. "I've got the S. Jeez, there's a boatload of Sumptners. No Erins, but several Es."

"Could you call them for me and see if one is an Erin Kelly Sumptner?"

"What am I supposed to say if I find her?"

"Give her my name and address and tell her I'm inquiring about purchasing the old log house on the Hill property in Wilson County."

"But I thought you bought a house."

"I did. And when do you plan to visit *me* for a change, hmmm?"

"Wait a minute. You're going to buy another house?"

"You know me, Chris. I get these bees in my bonnet and go off on my tangents. This house sits in back of mine, and the real estate agent said it was built a hundred years ago. I thought it might be fun to renovate it, though of course it's locked and I haven't seen the interior yet. But I'd like to. Tell the truth, it's driving me crazy, not being able to snoop around inside."

"Okay, I'll try. What day and time do you want me to show up at the Sheraton with a gargantuan appetite?"

As Meg hung up, she caught herself wishing once again that Chris didn't live so far away. Three or four years could go by between the times they saw one another for a few hours and tried to catch up on their separate lives.

With her finely-honed sense of the utter absurdity of life, Chris had a special talent for making Meg feel sane.

Since she'd last talked face-to-face with her best friend, Meg had finally worked up her nerve and suffered through the inevitable but nasty divorce from Jack. She'd met another man and fallen in love and then buried Warren.

And somehow, despite all of that, she'd seen Jenny through high school graduation.

And managed to use most of her paltry final divorce settlement to buy a house.

It didn't seem possible. Where had the years gone?

Chapter Nine

Despite the furnace thermostat turned to seventy-five degrees, the house remained drafty.

Each night during a three-day cold snap, Meg bundled up in flannel nightgown, two sweaters, and insulated socks with bedroom slippers, reminding her of the residents at the local nursing home whenever she caught a glimpse of herself in the floor-length mirror. The only item missing to complete the disturbing portrait was a neon-orange crocheted afghan.

But she could at least appreciate her ash-brown hair. After a couple of shampoos, the color seemed natural. "Chris, eat your heart out," she'd say to her friend, who had let her hair turn salt-and-pepper years ago and wore it as short as she could manage and still have hair.

Cherry Lamb slept near a furnace vent and never moved. Even Bart, Cappy, and Babu seem sluggish, preferring to curl up in warm places instead of entertaining themselves with their customary feline disagreements that generally made their mistress lose patience with the lot of them.

Meg put extra blankets on her bed, but after the third morning of waking up to a chilly house and having to tip-toe on an ice-cold linoleum floor to reach the coffee pot, the temperamental furnace had gotten on her nerves. She could hear it turn on, then the blower would start. After a few minutes the furnace shut itself off before much heat had a chance to rise through the floor-vents.

She tried to get a service man out to the house, calling from her office only to find that the two men renowned for their crafty repair skills who lived in Wilson were both recently retired. Someone from miles away would need to be scheduled, entailing a hefty service charge for merely appearing at her door.

She told the last person she'd spoken to that she'd have to think about it. A major repair bill before Christmas was no doubt looming in the near financial future. County employees were paid on the last working day of the month, and Meg's September paycheck had been well-consumed.

Thursday she took two hours of annual leave, stopped by the store to stock up on Halloween candy since Wilson had moved the holiday from mid-week to Saturday night, and arrived home early. Planning to take advantage of the last hours of daylight, she changed into a ragged pair of jeans and a sweatshirt and hauled the wooden ladder from the outdoor shed into her bedroom.

Emptying the closet of clothes, she cleared the boarded-up entrance to the attic located in the ceiling of the closet. Propping the ladder against the wall required removing the clothes bar. Otherwise, her weight on the ladder would break it, and then where would she be?

She went down to the basement and found the hammer and flashlight.

After pounding on the clothes bar with the hammer, she managed to loosen the bar at one end and let it fall to the floor at an angle. Positioning the ladder, she climbed up three rungs and pressed against the board blocking the entrance. It appeared to be nailed shut.

Holding the flashlight with her left hand, she pulled out two nails on each side with the claws of the hammer. When she pushed on the board, it fell all at once, causing her to teeter precariously on the ladder.

Setting the board aside, she trained the beam of the flashlight into the hole. Was it wide enough for her fleshy middle-aged hips to squeeze through?

She reached up to set the flashlight on the attic floor, climbed another rung of the ladder, and poked her head into the opening to look around.

Well, the attic was insulated, all right, the underside of the roof coated with lengths of pink fiberglass that seemed in good condition. She switched off the flashlight to see slats of late- afternoon sunlight shining through the ventilation window at the west attic dormer.

Sunlight caught the metal clasp of an old trunk pushed under the eaves at the far end of the house. To whom had it belonged? From the tumbleweeds of dust and dead insects on the floor, it looked as though no one had been up here in years.

Meg pulled herself onto the floor hoping it would support her weight and took the flashlight to investigate. The metal clasp was not fastened. Crouching so as not to hit her head on the roof beams, she opened the lid of the trunk.

Stacks of clothing were neatly folded. A black gabardine dress from the 'Fifties, with a whirling Loretta Young skirt, white Peter Pan collar and cuffs. Examining the other items, Meg concluded that the black dress was the prize, for the rest could have gone into a rag bag. Old print dresses of thin cotton suitable for a farmer's wife canning tomatoes in a sweltering kitchen. Several pairs of cotton Bermudas, a few blouses.

But at the bottom she found two shoeboxes filled with someone's papers. She replaced the clothing in the trunk and carried the shoeboxes with her as she crawled through the opening and carefully eased down the ladder.

She replaced the board and nailed it shut with the original nails. Then she hammered the clothes bar into its slot, gathered her clothing from the bed, and hung it up.

After hauling the ladder back to the shed, Meg returned to the house, taking the shoeboxes to the kitchen table for a leisurely inspection of their contents.

As a child, she had loved Nancy Drew books, and she almost felt as she had then, following the exploits of the girl detective. She hoped a clue in these postcards and letters would tell her something of the former inhabitants of her house.

The widow who had died in her house, Faith Fleming Hill, was Melody Hill Branscombe's mother. But why would Melody have left her mother's things in this house before it was placed on the market? Had she not known the trunk was stored in the attic? Or had her memory already begun to deteriorate by the time her mother passed away?

The telephone rang at twenty minutes before six.

"Mom? Joe moved out of the trailer," Jenny said. "Just wanted you to know. Brianna's mother nearly made her move back home when she found out he was living here."

Meg gave the woman credit for not mentioning they'd talked, for that would have been the first thing Jenny said. "Jenny, are you calling from the trailer?"

"They put in the phone today. Want to jot down the number?"

"Is it listed in your name?"

"I had to put it in my name. I'm the only one working full time."

Meg sighed. "Jenny, every time I talk to you, something else comes up. You told me Brianna and Nell were working at the garment factory."

"Uh, Nell quit because she couldn't stand the supervisor. She's looking for another job. But they cut back Brianna's hours, so she's going out on interviews for a new job, too."

"Jenny, I love you, but so help me, I'll not finance that trailer for you and your friends. Frankly, I can't. And there's no way you can pay the rent and all the bills on your salary from Burger Master."

"I know, Mom," Jenny said wearily. "I worked twelve hours today alone. I feel like I'm going to fall asleep on my feet that are throbbing like a toothache. And I have to open at four a.m. tomorrow, too. It's really getting to be a drag."

Good. "Then I'll let you go so you can get your rest. Try soaking your feet in Epsom salts. Keep in touch."

"You, too. Love you."

Had she detected a slight note of homesickness in Jenny's voice? No, probably not. Wishful thinking.

She gave her pets their dinner, found a casual outfit to wear to the office the next day, thankfully a Friday, and took a bath. For dinner, Meg boiled a package of Ramen noodles without adding the salty flavor packet and ate in the living room while watching the evening news, the thermostat of the furnace set at eighty. Though the overnight low would be forty degrees, the temperature in her house remained frigid.

Had her life come to this at age fifty, huddled in flannel with only her cats and an aged dog for company? Evidently, it had.

If she wasn't careful, the next thing she knew, Meg Kites would be eating little bowls of warm, nourishing porridge. But this bowl of noodles was close. Suddenly she lost her appetite.

Defiantly, she lit a cigarette and inhaled deeply. She didn't want to live to be ninety-five anyway, only to end up an addle-brained, drooling old woman in Somerset Manor with a Christmas package of butterscotch candy as the only bright spot to look forward to.

She switched off the television, let the cats out, and settled down at the kitchen table to winnow through Faith Hill's papers.

Either Faith Hill had been a well-organized woman, or Melody had arranged things chronologically at some point in her life before her powers of concentration departed. The first box had postcards from faraway places, from major cities all over the United States but mostly out west. Some of these were so old they might well have been collector's items. Arizona desert at sunset. The Alamo. Golden Gate Bridge.

Each card was addressed to Mr. and Mrs. Lucas Hill. A message of a line or two about the weather. Signed, Caleb Hill.

Meg reached for the notepad and pen and started a family tree. Lucas was married to Faith, and their daughter Melody married someone named Branscombe. Who was Caleb Hill? A brother to Lucas?

A Christmas card dated 1897. In a woman's hand, "Our first Christmas as husband and wife. Please grace us with your blessings. Lucy and Caleb."

Caleb was married to Lucy.

But where did Erin Kelly Sumptner fit into the picture?

Deep among chatty letters written to Faith by various women signed only with first names – she had not been one to keep envelopes – was a small box of stationery still emitting a faint scent of perfume. Apparently never used, or so Meg thought when she opened the box to blank sheets of paper. On closer scrutiny, toward the middle of the paper were several sheets filled with a woman's handwriting.

"I fear I have driven a wedge between Lucas and Caleb. I warned him not to marry her. She has brought nothing but grief to this family. August 8, 1899."

"I know that in his own way Lucas loves me. What he has done,

God forgive his soul, he did for me. But in my heart I will always know he loved her more. She was but thirty years of age, and now she is gone forever. I fear Caleb will not endure this. I am so fearful that sleep will not come to me. I am gravely ill. April 15, 1905.”

"Their home has been sealed, with memories of their brief life together contained within. I am sending a few mementos to Lucy's sister Catherine in Richmond, but all else has been left intact for Melody to find someday. Lucas arranged a memorial service for Caleb. He has said Caleb was killed in a railroad riot in Montana. It had been longer than eight months since he disappeared. What has happened to Caleb is unlikely ever to be known. November 24, 1916."

"And now that I am an old woman, he has come to haunt me. I know he wants me to reveal the truth to Melody. I cannot. It would break her spirit, I fear. Too many years have passed, and she is truly my daughter now. I find myself waiting, searching for him. I must solve this mystery before I die. I shall not pen my thoughts again. January 8, 1962. FRH."

A span of over sixty years between the first and fourth entries!

Meg rifled through the remaining papers, her curiosity piqued to learn more, but the trail grew cold. A recipe for peanut soup, several yellowing magazine articles, one on childcare, two about planning a seaside vacation. She saved Faith's remarks in the original stationery box, together with the family tree she had tried to trace.

What mystery had obsessed Faith Hill? And whom had she believed haunted her in her old age? What truth had she refused to tell Melody? And from what she had written, was Melody not Faith's own biological daughter?

She is truly my daughter now; what woman who was a child's natural mother would have written those words in exactly that way? Meg couldn't imagine.

But of one thing she felt certain. Faith Hill had also been connected to the history of the old log house, so much so that she had purchased Meg's house after it was built in 1940, and she had lived here until her death. Why?

At eleven o'clock, Meg tried to sleep. When she thought of calling

Richmond in the morning for dates of birth and death, at last she could let herself rest.

It was noon on Friday before Meg finally devised a devious strategy to find out what she needed to know. Technically, the Bureau of Vital Statistics in Richmond was not permitted to give out details concerning specific people without a written request, but Meg said she represented the Wilson County Genealogical Society. In less than five minutes on the phone, she had written down several important dates to add to her Hill chronology.

Lucas Hill, born Wilson County 1854, died 1930; Faith Rebecca Hill, born Faith Rebecca Fleming 1865, place unknown, died 1962 Wilson County; Caleb Hill, born Wilson County 1869, died 1916 Billings, Montana. Melody Hill, born 1900 Wilson County. No record of Lucy Hill's birth or death.

"But she died in Wilson County in 1905, according to our records here," Meg protested.

"I'm sorry, but a death certificate was never filed with the Bureau through the Wilson County coroner."

"Could you give me the date of marriage?"

"We don't have that information. You'll have to check with the Clerk's office at the County Courthouse if the marriage took place in Wilson County."

All at once Meg remembered Faith's statement about sending a few things to Lucy's sister Catherine in Richmond. Could Catherine have been Erin Sumptner's mother? If so, Meg was beginning to make some sense from so many unraveled threads that somehow linked the people who were the Hill clan, all of it leading to one ancient woman in the Somerset Manor nursing home.

Well, that was enough digging for one day. Meg tucked the notes she'd made into her purse, and turned her attention to incoming correspondence, including an official communique on letterhead with the County seal from the County Manager, relaying Board approval for Norman Feder's official reclassification.

Praise the Lord!

Chapter Ten

Cappy was overdue for his combination shot, and Cherry Lamb's incontinence had escalated to a level beyond Meg's tolerance. At nine o'clock Saturday morning, she waited at the clinic located in downtown Wilson for her veterinarian to arrive.

Well past usual retirement age, Dr. Mitchum maintained his practice on a part-time schedule. When he finally did retire, Meg wondered whether she could afford to keep all of her animals. He was the only reasonable vet in the county, not to mention the wisest and most experienced. There didn't seem to be a single animal malady that he couldn't diagnose and treat.

By nine-fifteen, Dr. Mitchum's Jeep rolled up, and he waved at her to come through the front entrance.

"Who needs what today?" he asked Meg.

"I called your receptionist Wednesday. She says Cappy is due for the combination."

She pulled him gently from his cat taxi and he trembled in her hands. She imagined the poor little guy remembered staying here for nearly a week several years ago, when the vet had saved his life from a dire case of feline urinary tract disorder. But today Dr. Mitchum gave him two shots, and Meg pushed Cappy into the pet carrier. If cats could communicate, she was sure she saw relief in those sparkling green eyes.

"I have to take him out to the car and bring my dog in. She's the one who's fifteen and wets. I've been putting disposable diapers on her at night."

"I can probably fix that with a little female hormone. Not too much, though, or all the boys in the neighborhood will be over, thinking she's in heat."

When Meg took the pet carrier out to the car, four cars were lined up, the occupants waiting their turn. She put Cappy in the hatch and dragged Cherry Lamb on a leash to the clinic.

"Dr. Mitchum, why does she have all these bald spots? She's eating herself to death."

"Fleas, plain and simple. Even one flea will drive a dog crazy. I have some spray that gets rid of fleas in the next county. You hold her muzzle." When he began spraying, fleas jumped off the dog onto the examining table.

"But I give her a flea bath once a week. I don't understand how she still has fleas."

"Here, take this home and use it. Then put Sevin-Dust around the house, anywhere the dog goes. Now keep holding her and I'll inject a little hormone."

"Should I continue putting diapers on her at night?"

"Oh, yes, indeed. If they're dry in a couple of weeks, call me and I'll prescribe a pill for you to mash in her food on a regular basis. If this works."

"And you said male dogs might come around, even though she's spayed?"

"If I give her too much. They won't know she's spayed till they get there."

"Hmmm. Wonder if that would work for me."

Dr. Mitchum chuckled. "If it did, I imagine I'd be a mighty rich man."

Meg waited while the vet figured her bill. Writing a check, she said, "Dr. Mitchum, you said you were born and raised right here in Wilson County."

"Sure was. In a house down Main Street, still standing. Another family has it now, though."

"Do you remember the name Hill? Lucas and Caleb Hill?"

For a few seconds the elderly gentleman gazed off into the distance. "Sure does ring a bell. Haven't thought about them for years. There was one strange story, too."

"Oh? How so?"

70

"They were brothers, different as daylight and dark. Lucas was a right successful attorney in town, had a flourishing practice. His wife, her name was..." He snapped his fingers, trying to recall.

"Faith?"

"That's right! Faith. She and my mother were friends, they played canasta and bridge with some other ladies. So I heard things from Mother that Faith might have told her in confidence, I don't know. But all of them are long dead now, so I guess it doesn't matter."

"Please tell me!" She didn't want to be obnoxious or pushy, but Meg suspected she'd tapped a goldmine.

"Well, Faith hired this pretty little Irish girl, an immigrant she was, brogue and all. And Caleb took a shine to her. In those days people of Faith's social status looked down their patrician noses at people fresh off the boat, so to speak. So Faith hired this girl for her domestic, and less than a year later Caleb up and married her. She was a looker, too. Lucy, her name was. They had some children, as I recollect, but I don't know whether any of them survived."

"So Lucy wasn't born in this country?"

"No. At least that's what Mother said. Didn't die here, either. That's the strange part of the story. One day she left, and no one ever heard from her again. A few years later, Caleb perished out west, something to do with violence. I was a young boy, but I remember going to the funeral service for Caleb. They buried an empty coffin up in the cemetery on the hill here in town. Faith told my mother she believed Caleb died of a broken heart."

"Dr. Mitchum, did you know Melody Hill Branscombe?"

"Faith's daughter. She's still living, isn't she? Seems I heard from somebody she's out at the nursing home."

"Yes, she is. I went to visit her briefly. She's ninety-five, and not well."

"Well, she married a young man from Lexington and lived there for a number of years. They never had children from what I understand. After her husband passed on, she came home to Wilson and lived with her mother. Then Faith died, and Melody was placed in the nursing home shortly thereafter."

Two people had ventured into the outer office. An English bulldog yipped at a Chihuahua.

"I'd better go and let you treat the next patient. Thank you, Dr. Mitchum. I've enjoyed talking with you." *More than you know*, she thought to herself.

Meg took Cappy and Cherry home and quickly jotted down the information she had gathered from Dr. Mitchum.

Gradually, the Hill chronology was beginning to flesh out.

****

Wichita, Kansas, 1916, the circus arrived for a week's stay shortly before Thanksgiving.

Honora, the new assistant, turned the cabinet clockwise on sturdy casters. With a radiant stage-smile, she threw open the doors.

From the crowd came a gasp. A woman screamed.

Two burning-red eyes flashed from within the dark enclosure. The horned, hairy creature crouched in the cabinet resembled nothing human.

Quickly, the assistant bolted the doors and spun the cabinet in the opposite direction, desperately calling his name.

He saw her through a veil, as if a caul had fallen over his face. He cried out to her, but she could not hear. His hands were unable to touch her. He could not break through the barrier from the other side.

The cabinet was destroyed with sledgehammers and fire, pronounced an evil gateway to Hell by the Topeka clergy.

And with the destruction of the cabinet, his portal to the earthly plane vanished in splinters and smoke.

Chapter Eleven

Only late in the day did Meg remember she'd neglected to check the mailbox.

When she came home from the vet's office, she threw a chuck roast in the Crock-pot with a can of mushroom soup, garlic cloves, a few peppercorns, bay leaf, and an envelope of French onion soup mix. At three p.m., she telephoned Jenny and invited the three girls to come for dinner.

She steamed broccoli with lemon-butter sauce and made twice-baked potatoes with a fluffy sour cream and cheese topping, angel-food cake with fresh strawberries and whipped cream for dessert.

At four, the girls appeared, Jenny dressed in her Burger Master uniform. By five o'clock, half the roast was consumed and the remainder packed in Tupperware for the trio of roommates to take home.

"Brianna seems to be sulking," Meg whispered to Jenny as they cleared the table. Nell and Brianna were in the living room watching a Madonna video on MTV.

"She'll get over it. I'm glad Joe's gone. He was really a slob. He peed all over the toilet seat and never cleaned it off." Jenny wrinkled her nose in disgust.

"I'm pleased to hear Brianna's mother actually gave a hoot about her daughter's living situation. Some parents could care less, these days. You don't know how many women my age have told me we can't tell our kids a thing. Just throw up your hands and let everything slide to hell. That seems to be the prevalent attitude." Meg washed dishes while Jenny dried. "Want me to pack the rest of those potatoes? They'll reheat in a slow oven if you cover them with foil."

"Would you? They were super. Mom, can I get some stuff from

the bathroom, too?”

“Help yourself. Just leave me one of whatever so I’m not stranded until I go to the store.”

“We’re even out of toilet paper.”

“I have lots. Take an eight-pack.”

“Thanks.” Jenny kissed her cheek. “And by the way. Dinner was scrumptious. Thanks for inviting us.”

“Anytime. You know I still consider this your home.”

Meg dried her hands on a dish towel and waited until Jenny returned from the bathroom with a loaded grocery bag.

“Honey, since it’s supposed to sleet tonight, the local radio station said they’ve moved Halloween to Monday, so I’m leaving the office a little early to stop for a few groceries. Due to the time change, the kids will be trick-or-treating by six, and I want to be here.”

“I’d like to be here, too, to help you give out the treats. But I have to work tonight, and Monday’s the last chance to see the Haunted House.”

“My next suggestion goes down the tube, then. I was going to ask you to help me. But seeing as how that’s out, here’s the next favor. I have to leave for Richmond on Thursday and I won’t be home Friday until well after nightfall. You’ll have to stay here Thursday night and care for the animals.”

“Can Nell stay, too?”

Meg gave Jenny a look. “Why? So Joe can stay at the trailer with Brianna?”

Jenny averted her eyes. “Mom, I can’t help what the two of them do. Don’t hold me responsible, please.”

“But this puts me in a bind, don’t you understand? What if her mother finds out?”

“Brianna’s eighteen.”

“And? Being eighteen doesn’t give you the keys to the Magic Kingdom.”

Jenny laughed. “No. Being eighteen gives you the keys to Burger Master so you get to open at four a.m.”

“I’m just glad it isn’t you who’s involved with Joe. Tell the truth,

I didn't care for the boy. He seems so sneaky, with those shifty eyes."
Should she add lazy, as well? "Incidentally, does he have a job?"

"No, and he's not in school, either. Joe has absolutely no
ambition. Frankly, Mom, I don't know what Brianna sees in him."

"My sentiments, exactly."

"But she says she's in love."

"Then let's hope she doesn't get herself pregnant."

Meg walked them out to Nell's Escort, grateful that Jenny wouldn't
be driving her Mazda in the sleet. After hearing the weather forecast,
she'd had the presence of mind to arrange a ride to the trailer from another evening-shift worker with a four-wheel-drive vehicle.

Meg checked the mailbox after they'd driven away. At ten minutes
till six, it was twilight. Though she enjoyed the extra hour of daylight in
the morning, she hated to see darkness come so early, but she realized
that in the winter you couldn't have it both ways.

She placed the mail on the kitchen counter before using the bathroom. She had to smile; Jenny had taken her instructions literally. On
the shelf was one shampoo, one conditioner, one disposable razor. At
least she hadn't wanted Meg's magic beauty lotion.

Telephone bill, a printed message from her Congressman, cable
TV bill, and a letter with a Richmond postmark. She ran her fingernail
beneath the flap and ripped it open.

2040 Grove Avenue
Richmond, VA. 23220
(804) 359-3281
October 23

Dear Meg Kites:

*I am the Erin Sumptner you were seeking. I've met your
delightful friend, Christine Phlegar, who said you are interested in the
log house belonging to my cousin, Melody H. Branscombe. Chris tells
me you will be in Richmond toward the end of next week. Please get in
touch while you are here, and come for tea.*

In hopes this letter will arrive on Saturday, and should time

75

permit, you could do me a great service. Would you be so kind as to inventory the contents of the log house, and perhaps bring it with you when we meet? A key to the house has always been hidden behind a dark-gray stone near the base of the chimney. A few drops of household oil in the lock of the front door might be called for.

My cousin has not been well for some time. I manage her affairs as best I can from such a distance. I am eighty-three years of age and have never learned to drive an automobile and doubt whether I shall, at my age.

Catherine Kelly, my mother, was the sister of Lucy Kelly Hill. Although to my knowledge, Melody was never told, Lucy and Caleb were Melody's parents, but she was taken in by Lucas and Faith Hill following the terrible tragedy. It is a sad story, and happened very long ago.

In any case, I have some of my aunt's papers, sent by Faith Hill to my mother after Lucy's death. Chris tells me you're an avid history buff, so you might have some use for them. I look forward to visiting with you soon.

Sincerely,
Erin K. Sumptner

Meg read the letter a second time and felt as though destiny had brushed her cheek. Erin Sumptner sounded sharp as a tack. She couldn't wait to meet the lady.

She took Faith's stationery box from a dresser drawer, looked at the rudimentary family tree she had sketched, considered the discrepancies heard from two different sources in a single day, and understood that an historical drama was unfolding before her eyes.

And a key to the old house, hidden in the chimney!

Impulsively, she picked up the phone and dialed Chris's number to thank her for locating Erin, but there was no answer after seven rings. She realized that she was unable to visualize Chris's empty apartment, for though the phone number was always the same, Chris was forever on the move, whittling her possessions in a compulsive residential downsizing.

She had divorced Allison's father when her daughter was five and, despite a few serious affairs, Chris had opted not to remarry. For twenty-five years now, Chris's one eccentricity was her adamant refusal to put down permanent roots.

Meg studied the notes she'd made while talking with the staff person at the Bureau of Vital Statistics. Melody was born in 1900, and Faith Hill's personal remarks mentioned Lucy's death in 1905 at age thirty, although there was no record of her death at the State Health Department. Both Erin Sumptner and Faith Hill had known of Lucy's death, yet Dr. Mitchum and probably the rest of the townspeople believed Lucy simply left town. Cole Mitchum wouldn't have told her so, had it not been the local perception.

Meg wondered which version Lucas and Faith Hill had given the bereaved Caleb Hill, the husband Faith believed had died of a broken heart.

And Faith had written of a memorial service for Caleb, revealing that Lucas manufactured a violent death for Caleb during a railroad riot in Montana. Or was it Dr. Mitchum who spoke of that? But she did remember the elderly veterinarian saying an empty coffin was buried in the town cemetery.

He also told Meg that Caleb and Lucy had several children, but he couldn't remember whether any had survived. But if Lucy died when Melody was five years old, how could Melody not have remembered Lucy as her mother? Or had Faith somehow managed to expunge the truth from the child's memory?

What secrets had been buried with the Hill family? Why the elaborate charade about death and disappearance? Why had the identity of her natural parents never been revealed to Melody Hill Branscombe?

And why had Faith Hill emphasized that the log house had been *sealed*?

How many years must have gone by, since anyone unlocked the door of the log house and ventured inside!

I must solve this mystery before I die. Meg was beginning to understand Faith Hill's obsession, if not the reasons for it. According to Faith's death certificate, she died in 1962, the same year she'd written about *him* coming to haunt her.

Who? The man in the black waistcoat Meg had seen on a country road?

Had her own visitant been Caleb Hill, who disappeared while searching for Lucy, believing she was still alive?

Ouch! She rubbed her arms rapidly. All of this speculation about strange events buried in the past had given her goosebumps.

Anxious to find the key, explore the old house, and complete the requested inventory for Erin Sumptner, she went to bed at ten o'clock.

****

Though she was disappointed by the dreary Sunday morning with a distinct possibility of either more sleet or rain, undaunted, Meg dressed warmly. Armed with a Thermos of black coffee, flashlight, notepad and pen, she arrived at the log house at eight a.m. Cherry Lamb had been left in the house, wearing one of her toddler-size Pampers.

Setting her things on the icy porch steps, Meg put on her gardening gloves and went to the chimney. Toward the base, a dark-gray stone. There it was, toward the house, in the back, the only stone in the beige river-rock chimney of that description and there was no mistaking it.

Meg tried to pull the stone away from its mooring, but evidently the years had securely cemented it in place. She searched for a stick and found a sturdy stalk from a catnip plant in the dried grass. With a few minutes of scraping around the edges and alternately tugging at the stone, it moved a fraction of an inch. Gradually, she was making it come loose.

She continued wheedling away at the crevices surrounding the stone until she could pull it free. An old-fashioned key rested in a natural fissure of the lower stone.

She replaced the dark-gray stone and took the key to the porch. Opening the screen door, the screening rusted away long ago, she inserted the key in the lock to the sound of rust or metal filings breaking up in the opening. Easily, the key turned the tumbler and the door opened grudgingly with one push on its frame. Meg switched on the flashlight and stepped into a uniform, lumpy darkness.

The shutters at the windows completely blocked out the natural light. She pushed up the wooden bar of the window nearest the door and pulled open the wooden panels to let in the light. A musty odor from the closed-up house forced her outside for a breath of fresh air.

But when she gazed at the room and its furnishings, Meg had the uncanny feeling that she had opened a time capsule. Everything had been draped in muslin. Coughing, she gathered up the lengths of fabric and piled them in a corner.

Antique American oak or pine furniture, handmade. A hutch with bubbled-glass door panels, bookshelves, a small writing desk with closed lid, several chairs with dusty brocade upholstery.

And the room's centerpiece, an ornately-carved Victorian sofa of burgundy velvet in pristine condition, the likes of which she'd never expected to see except at an estate sale or a shop dealing in vintage antiques.

Braided rugs. A wood stove vented into the chimney. An antique clock over the fireplace mantel. On the walls, a Civil War lithograph and a gushingly romantic, turn-of-the-century print of children presided over by a governess having a picnic on a riverbank.

Meg shone the flashlight on the books. Leather-bound works on Confederate subjects related to the Civil War. Books on Indian wars, naval history, explorers and settlers. A book on Gladstone, a British statesman.

Wallace's *Ben Hur*. Bushnell's *Christian Nurture*. She slid it from the shelf and flipped through the pages: a didactic book on child-rearing. A stack of magazines called *Godey's Lady's Book* contained stodgy articles about proper decorum and etiquette.

A book entitled *The Struggle for Immortality* by Elizabeth Stuart Phelps, 1889, that was inscribed on its fly sheet: "To my dearest sister Lucy, from Catherine. I trust this book will give you solace and comfort on the death of your infant son. My prayers remain with you and your husband and daughter."

Replacing the book on the shelf, Meg proceeded to the right into another room. A handmade cradle with a small patchwork quilt sat in one corner. An oak table and four chairs. Pewter candlesticks.

On a sideboard was an arrangement of skeleton leaves beneath a glass dome, with miniature pinecones and polished stones nestled under the artistic leaf patterns. Meg had seen something similar, though not nearly as impressive, at a crafts fair.

The woman at the booth had explained that leaf skeletons were a Victorian invention made by soaking dried leaves in water and then carefully scrubbing them with a brush until only the delicate veins of the leaf remained, apparently quite an art requiring patience and a light touch.

Had Lucy Hill created this?

Above the sideboard, a punched-paper design for needlework read *May the Good Lord Bless our Happy Home*.

The kitchen, off to the left, included an ancient wood cook-stove, a porcelain sink, and enamelware pots and pans. Meg didn't know much about rural living in nineteenth-century America, but she was interested in finding out how Lucy had kept her butter from turning rancid without refrigeration. In the far corner sat an oval tub with straight sides – the bathing tub? She couldn't fathom the energy required to fill it with buckets of water carried from the stream.

She returned to the living room, her enthusiasm having waned. It was just an old house filled with ordinary things. What had she expected?

The soft sound of a music box overhead; she must have jarred the mechanism by walking across the wooden floor. She turned toward the fireplace and the steep, narrow stairs leading to the second floor.

At the top of the stairs she was greeted by a beautiful creature with blue eyes and deep red hair, an oil portrait of a woman with a tiny, corseted waist in a brown velvet dress with faceted metal buttons, holding a bouquet of what appeared to be gardenias.

Hair piled atop her head in a Gibson-girl style, faint freckles dotting the bridge of her nose, her eyes fastened proudly on the artist who had painted the portrait. With her red hair and fair complexion, she looked Irish through and through. This was Lucy Hill, and there'd been nothing shy or retiring about Lucy. Had this been her formal wedding portrait?

No wonder Caleb Hill had been smitten by Lucy Kelly. She was utterly gorgeous.

There were two bedrooms, one filled with a little girl's things. A set of Brownie books! Meg's grandmother had read some of her own Brownie books to her, stories about magical elves Meg had loved. An antique doll with a porcelain, hand-painted face. A large dollhouse with Victorian furniture whose little people were missing. A carved wooden rocking-horse.

When Meg explored the second room, she felt like a spy. On a large vanity table with an oval mirror now streaked gray, beside the telltale music box was a large box of silver-plate shaped like a small chest. Inside she found an antique amethyst and diamond ring. She slipped it onto her ring finger. A perfect fit.

A pin-cushion of polished cotton or chintz with Virginia Beach spelled in dark-blue glass beads. Ivory and silver hair combs. A small conch-shell with a pearly pink interior. Meg held it to her ear as Lucy may have done so long ago, to listen to a faraway sea.

A cameo on a strip of black velvet with a tiny clasp. A gold locket containing a strand of fine, strawberry-blond baby hair tied with blue silk thread. Meg felt as if she might cry.

She moved back from the vanity table and its large oval mirror to leave the room. On a low wooden trunk sat a wooden Irish lap-harp and a pair of black ballet slippers with ankle straps, the leather brittle with age.

A bicycle with rubber wheels was propped against the far wall, a woman's bicycle. A tarnished brass plate beneath the seat read Victor, 1889.

Flooded with sadness, she walked down the stairs to the living room. Taking the notepad, she retraced her steps from room to room, noticing things she had not seen at first, such as the English Delftware in the hutch, a man's pipe in the writing desk. She wrote down each item in the house, every piece of furniture, the titles of the books, and the silver-ware in the drawer of the hutch, omitting nothing.

When she was ready to leave, she considered closing the shutters on the windows. But the glass panes would keep the weather out. It seemed too tragic to close the shutters again. Nor did she have the heart to replace the muslin.

Glancing around one last time, Meg closed the door and locked it. Then she replaced the key under the stone in the chimney and returned to her house.

At quarter past eleven, guiltily she thought of the church service she'd missed.

Though she had much to accomplish before the end of the day, none of it seemed high priority. And besides, she had one of those bees in her bonnet. There was one thing Meg felt compelled to do.

She scraped the ice from her car windows and drove to the cemetery that sat high on a knoll overlooking the town. The wrought-iron gates were open, and Meg drove through.

She soon discovered that the earliest graves were toward the back of the cemetery. After a great deal of walking and searching, she found the headstones for Lucas and Faith Hill, beside the monument for Caleb Hill with dates of birth and death, and the infant son Ian Caleb Hill, with only one date: October 3, 1903. Then the baby had been stillborn.

Dark clouds tufted the sky. A wintry wind whistled through the trees, swirling eddies of dry leaves over the graves at Meg's feet. An eerie feeling descended upon her. Because she had previously learned the dates of birth and death on the gravestones before she'd ever visited the cemetery, she almost felt as if she'd been here before.

To the grave of Caleb Hill, she said, "Whatever it is you're looking for, I'll try to find it for you. If it's the mystery of what happened to Lucy, well, I'd like to know that, too."

As if in response, the wind moaned through the cemetery, creaking the limbs of a bare dogwood tree at her side.

She felt very foolish, speaking to a marble slab and a mound of earth, but her sentiments had been genuine. At last she turned away and walked to her car.

With laundry to do and nylons to wash, Meg occupied herself for the remainder of that bleak Sunday in a daze, her mind unaware of what her hands were doing. She couldn't contain her curiosity to know more, her thoughts revolving around the pieces of a puzzle that slowly seemed to fit together.

She imagined the sort of life Lucy Hill had lived in the old log house. In those days, women washed clothes by hand in tubs with water boiled on the stove. Meals were made from scratch, shopping an almost daily occurrence for women who didn't live on a farm. Housecleaning was a constant occupation, and with no modern conveniences. To Meg's mind, Lucy's life qualified as one of certifiable drudgery.

What kind of love had they shared, Caleb and Lucy Hill? Certainly not the brand of disappointment Meg had twice experienced.

For dinner, she hopped in the car and drove through Burger Master for a double cheeseburger, fries, and a diet cola. Working the drive-through window, when she saw her mother, Jenny flashed a bright smile.

As she drove home, Meg realized that seeing Jenny had made her feel anchored to the real world again.

Later, as she was getting ready for bed, she heard the sound of a woman weeping, as distinctly as if someone had been crying in the next room. She flicked off the bedroom light, allowed her eyes to adjust to the sudden darkness, and peered through the window.

Again, the phantom light shone in the upstairs bedroom. What made it all the more peculiar now was Meg's careful morning inspection of the log home. There were no lights in the upstairs bedrooms, no candles, no kerosene lanterns or lamps. In fact, the entire house had been totally devoid of light.

And then she saw him in the glow from a half-moon, the man in black. He did not walk toward the log house, but drifted six inches from the ground.

A shudder ran through her, but Meg remained at the window. What had she untapped by opening the door of the old house, by allowing the present to ooze into the past?

Then, with a shock, Meg realized she still wore Lucy's amethyst and diamond ring.

Chapter Twelve

After an early-morning call to Jenny on Thursday as a reminder to feed the pets, she gave a reassuring pat to each of her cats and to Cherry Lamb before leaving the house. A suitcase with her nightgown, underwear, and the conference ensemble, and a bag of jars containing Victory Garden Chili Sauce for Chris Phlegar, were in hand.

She deposited her car in the county parking lot behind the modern four-story courthouse and found the vehicle assigned to her for the trip. An '89 Crown Victoria recycled from the Sheriff's fleet, no handles on the inside of the back doors to discourage old ghosts of prisoners from trying to escape, ninety-thousand miles on the odometer. Empty spaces on the dashboard where the police CB and ashtray must have been. Not as new as the '94 sedan enjoyed by Mr. Feder, Meg thought to herself.

Whoever said bureaucrats at the local level wasted the taxpayers' money? She hoped she could get to Richmond and back without a major mechanical mishap.

Well, at least the heater and radio worked.

By ten o'clock she was on the road, a straight shot up interstate 81, past Lexington and Covington, up to Staunton to turn right on 64 East for a beeline to Richmond. Keeping the speed at 70, she made good time, enjoying the pastoral, picture-book farms on rolling fields green with winter wheat on either side of the eight-lane highway.

At the Waynesboro/Staunton exit, Meg turned off to gas up the car at a Shell station and to have a light lunch at the Shoney's restaurant salad bar, reminding herself to put the receipts in a safe place for reimbursement. Travel, food, and lodging was a skimpy line-item in this year's budget, as Meg was one of the few department heads who disdained all but the unavoidable conferences. But this one was a must, designed to impart the details of the Governor's workfare program for welfare recipients.

Just think of it! Mr. Feder could *nab 'em* and make them work for their pittance. Meg thought he'd have made an excellent slave-driver wielding a cat-o'-nine-tails in the galley of a Roman ship.

Perhaps he'd actually had such a role in a previous life. How else to explain his inordinate zeal for fraud investigation? Mr. Feder had evolved into a new incarnation, a man with a mission to protect the county from illegal claims.

Meg grinned as she remembered yesterday's desperate phone call from Marty Flynn, County Manager.

"He thinks I'm his boss! Practically every time I turn around, there he is again like a bad penny."

"Well, to sweeten the pot, Marty, I think I did insinuate he'd be dually supervised by me and thee."

"But he's a fanatic! You'd think those poor bastards he's after were serial killers!"

She couldn't resist. "No, they buy frozen crab legs and breeze off in Dodge Vipers."

"Meg, you're going to have to get this bozo off my ass."

"Why, you could do that, Marty. Remember what you said when I repeatedly complained to you about Norman Feder? You said it was simple as pie to get rid of him. Your exact words as I recall were document, document, document."

Marty's response? Slamming the phone down.

Really, no one could fault Mr. Feder's performance in his new position. The court case dockets were jammed with Mr. Feder's alleged cheaters. Clients claiming to have dependents that didn't exist was a big one. In his zeal to prosecute, he combed the shopping malls, supermarkets, department stores, searching endlessly for offenders worth flogging. Nights, weekends, holidays, he gave them no mercy.

She cruised into Richmond on the Powhite Parkway, getting off at the Carey Street exit to the Sheraton at the edge of downtown Richmond. She parked the car in the underground lot, took the elevator to the lobby, went to the front desk and checked in.

"Smoking or non-smoking?"

"Smoking." What had the management done, segregate the smokers in a special wing in case of fire, so they could all perish together? Shades of Hieronymus Bosch!

"Room three-ten," the young man behind the counter said officiously, young enough to be her son, scarcely older than Jenny. Strawberry-blond peach fuzz grew in abundance on his rosy, boyish cheeks.

On her way to the elevator, Meg waved to a few people she recognized, welfare directors from other parts of the state and all with hang-dog expressions. Oh, but this promised to be a dismal gathering. She'd be glad when it was over, six hours of monotonous discourse in a stifling room, reams of regulations in microscopic print.

The hotel clerk had given her a plastic card to be inserted in a special slot to gain admittance to her room. Meg slipped the card in and out a dozen times before the light flashed green and she could turn the doorknob. Another irritating offering of modern technology. She pushed the door open and surveyed her room.

Two double beds, dresser with color television. She could watch a newly released movie to the tune of an extra eight dollars added to her bill, which she'd have to pay out-of-pocket. The county didn't reimburse employees for anything smacking of recreation or enjoyment, including the forbidden treat of a cocktail at dinner. The women in Finance would be on her tail for an itemized receipt. In their own way, they were fraud investigators, too.

She unpacked the few things from her suitcase and hung the clothes in the closet, taking her cosmetics to the bathroom. A small coffee pot; she poured water through the machine, emptied a pouch of coffee into the basket, and turned it on to brew. Then she filled the bathtub, using a courtesy bath-salts to scent the water for a leisurely bath. She had a stiff neck and her bones ached from five hours of alert driving. It was only four o'clock, and Chris was to meet her in the lobby at five-thirty.

After she'd dressed and applied make-up, Meg sat down on one of the beds and dialed Erin Sumptner's number.

"Mrs. Sumptner? This is Meg Kites....Yes, I just got into town.

I'm at my hotel. When could you see me?....No, I have to be home tomorrow night, so Saturday's out. How about tomorrow afternoon, around two or three? I promise not to stay long, but I did bring the inventory you asked for....Yes, I'm familiar with Richmond. I used to live here. I know where you live, close to Fox Elementary School....Thanks so much. I'll see you then."

It would be easy for Meg to duck out of the conference after lunch, which should get her to Grove Avenue by two p.m. and on her way home by three or four.

Stuffed into a basic black dress and green blazer, she took the elevator to the lobby at five-thirty to find Chris lounging in an easy chair, wearing faded jeans, tennis shoes, and an olive-drab sweater. "Feed me!" were Chris's first words.

Soon they were seated in the Sheraton restaurant, studying the menu. They agreed to the salad bar and noodles Alfredo. Chris ordered white wine, but Meg preferred hot tea.

"What's with you?" Chris asked. "Are you on the wagon? I never knew you to resist a glass of wine."

"You didn't see the way Warren died. It made me despise the scent of alcohol. Even wine."

"Then to change an unpleasant subject, let's talk about Erin Sumptner. What a cool old broad! I'm going to keep in touch with her. We met for lunch at the Art Museum. Then we looked around at the exhibits. She knows more about the French Impressionists than anyone outside Paris."

"I'm anxious to meet her." Meg told Chris of her plans to visit with Erin Sumptner the following afternoon.

"So what's all this business you're involved in, about the Hill family?"

They talked over dinner and raspberry sherbet for dessert, and it was ten o'clock before they realized that, once again, time had gotten away from them.

"I have to be going," Chris said. "But I really look forward to your letters. Write and tell me how the sleuthing works out, since you've fanned my curiosity to find out what really happened to Lucy."

"Well, I've been trying to prepare myself for the worst-case scenario, that we may never know."

Chris reached across the table and took Meg's right hand, turning it over to examine the palm. "Just promise me you won't get into your occult bullshit again. Remember when we took the kids to Myrtle Beach that summer and had our palms read? And my reading was out in left field but yours eventually came true?"

Meg pulled her hand back and stared at her palm. "You're right. It *did* come true, didn't it? The divorce, the second love lost, and a third love strong enough to last forever. Her exact words. I'd forgotten! At the time I was still madly in love with Jack, so I thought my reading was out in left field, too. But two out of three isn't bad. At least she got the first two right, the split with Jack, and then Warren's untimely demise."

"Hey, thanks for dinner and the chili sauce." Chris gave her a sisterly hug.

After a long night of tossing and turning in an unfamiliar bed with a firm mattress and a mushy pillow, Meg woke up in a grumpy mood. To make matters worse, the State Welfare Directors conference was even more stultifying than she'd feared. When her peers asked questions, Meg wanted to groan.

"Who cares?" she whispered to a plump woman sitting beside her. The woman looked at Meg with disapproval. "I don't know about you, but this happens to be my bread and butter."

"Oh. Sorry."

She skipped lunch, checked out and fled to the county car an hour early, a stack of papers tucked in her luggage. She planned to read through them over the weekend and have a report on Marty's desk by noon on Monday.

Not that he'd be inclined to read a single word of her report. She knew he only wanted it to protect his own behind, in the event one of the Board of Supervisors might ask a pertinent question related to implementation of the workfare program at the local level.

Workfare wasn't for the hapless participants, but for the middle-class taxpayers who had long frowned at the concept of a perpetual Giving Tree grafted to overburdened public coffers.

88

Which was precisely how Norman Feder had cadged his plum, made-to-order job as designated welfare fraud investigator, due to the decidedly mean-spirited mood of the times.

With a sigh, Meg loaded her suitcase in the trunk, and drove off to what she hoped would be a more fruitful experience.

Chapter Thirteen

At one o'clock, Meg parked at the curb in front of 2040 Grove Avenue. It was a slim three-story stone and brick house constructed near the turn of the century now painted Colonial blue, sandwiched between others of the same era. She collected her handbag from the passenger seat, walked up the sidewalk and rang the doorbell.

A tiny woman in a lacy beige dress, with blue hair and elaborate make-up, answered the door. "Are you Meg Kites?"

"And you're Erin Sumptner. So glad to meet you. Sorry I'm a little early."

"Do come in, dear."

Erin ushered her into the living room, chunky furniture from the 1940s that had recently come into vogue, yet Meg felt certain these items were vintage. Lace doilies sprinkled around the room and the lace curtains at the window gave the room a hushed, romantic quality harking back to bygone times.

"Chris Phlegar would so admire your living room," Meg said. "She loves furniture of this era."

"My first husband and I bought it when the both of you were babies," Erin said, taking a seat. "I liked your friend Chris very much. We spent a pleasant hour at the museum. Please, make yourself comfortable."

As she mentioned having dinner with Chris the previous night, Meg removed the folded pages from her handbag and gave them to Erin. "There's the inventory." She sat quietly while the woman read through it. When Erin looked up at her, Meg said, "I went to visit with your cousin at the nursing home recently."

"How kind of you to do that, Meg. Poor Melody. She was such

a lively, mischievous little red-haired girl, from her photographs. You'd never know, to see her now. I paid her a visit nearly four years ago, and it was quite an ordeal. I took the train to Roanoke and hired a limousine to drive me to Wilson. But she didn't remember me, didn't seem to have the slightest notion of who I could be. It made me sad to see her in such pitiful condition."

Meg nodded. "Erin, you said you had some of Lucy's papers. Do you remember her at all?"

"Only through my mother's memories. I never knew her. I was born ten years after Lucy's death, when my mother was thirty-five, in nineteen and fifteen."

Meg started to ask...well, why not? "Erin, would you mind if I took a few notes while we chat? For my own use, of course. Since I'm not a journalist or historian, certainly this will never see print. But I wondered if you could share anything that might tell me more about Lucy and her marriage to Caleb."

The woman studied Meg shrewdly. "Any special reason for asking, dear?"

"I think...well, it sounds crazy, but I think I may have seen the ghost of Caleb Hill."

Erin's fragile hand quivered at her throat. "Oh, my. You know, Mother told me on her death-bed about Caleb appearing to her in dreams. All this time I'd thought it was nothing but an elderly woman's imagination. The strangest thing! And now you believe you've seen his ghost. I suppose Mother may have been right, after all."

"What about, Erin?" Meg had her pen and paper at the ready.

"That Caleb would never give up until he found Lucy, even if it took all eternity."

And a third love strong enough to last forever; was this the third part of the palm reader's fortune?

"But you said Lucy died, and from what I can gather, Faith and Lucas told acquaintances in Wilson she'd simply disappeared."

"Well, they said as much to Caleb, too, and that was their mistake. As long as he believed she was alive, he searched for her. And when they realized their folly and tried to tell him she'd actually died, he was much past the point of believing them. He'd become utterly obsessed with finding her. Mother knew the story, though. Faith told her, on my mother's solemn vow never to reveal the truth to anyone, least of all to Caleb."

Quietly, Meg asked, "And what was the truth?"

Again, Erin Sumptner's bejeweled hand flew to her throat. "Faith told Mother that Lucy committed suicide and was buried in unhallowed ground, in an unmarked grave."

"Did your mother believe her sister took her own life?"

Huffily, Erin said, "Of course not. Catherine and Lucy Kelly were daughters of a minister. Suicide was a mortal sin damning a soul to everlasting Hell. According to Mother, Lucy would never have killed herself."

"You seem very sure."

"Well, I am. Oh, it's true, after her second child was stillborn, Lucy sank into a terrible depression. Mother said she worried herself sick over Lucy, but what could she do? Richmond was so far away from Wilson County. Imagine having to travel such a long distance in horse and buggy or a Model-T. But somehow she did manage to see Lucy twice after the child was buried, but not again before Faith wrote to her about Lucy's...death."

Meg mentioned Catherine's inscription in the book she had found in the old house.

"Of anything here," Erin said, looking at the inventory, "I'd like very much to have the book. If you wouldn't mind sending it to me."

"Of course. Erin, what did your mother tell you about Lucy? I mean, after all, they were sisters."

Erin's eyes sparkled. "How I wish I'd known her! Mother was the baby, the shy one. But Lucy? Full of fire. Though she and my mother came to this country and were hired out into homes as domestics, and mind you, this was over a century ago when women had few options, Lucy heartily resented women's secondary status. She loved to dance, when dancing was frowned upon as one of Satan's inventions. And she played the harp and sang old Gaelic airs she and Mother learned as children from their grandmothers in Ireland."

Erin paused, a faraway look in her watery blue eyes. "Everything

Lucy touched turned to gold, Mother said. She greatly admired Lucy. When Caleb asked her to marry him, there wasn't a thing Caleb's family could do to prevent it. Had the situation been reversed, a woman's family could have sent her away to Europe or to stay with distant relatives until the passion cooled and an acceptable suitor was found. But they couldn't very well do that with Caleb. According to my mother, Faith, Lucy's sister-in-law, never accepted Lucy into the family. It worsened when Caleb and Lucy went on the road with the traveling magic show."

"Magic show!"

"You don't know? Caleb's great love, next to Lucy, had always been magic. His brother persuaded him to go to the university in Charlottesville and find a respectable position in business with the railroad. But Lucy encouraged him to become a magician after they married. So Caleb tried to do both, which meant he was away from home much of the time, leaving Lucy alone with their small daughter. When her second child died, Lucy resorted to strange practices and medicines. I don't know the details, Mother preferred not to tell me, even when I pressed her as any normally-curious child would."

Meg's hand had dashed across the page, writing as much as she could. But then she sat back with a sigh. "This reveals yet another wrinkle in the tale," she said.

Erin glanced at the inventory. "What did you have in mind about the old house?"

"I thought I'd try to have it renovated. Put in a bathroom, have the house wired for electricity, eventually a furnace and insulation. Renting it out."

"My, wouldn't that be preferable to letting it sit there and fall to ruin? I'll call my attorney and see whether he can arrange an auction on Melody's death. There are acres and acres of land connected with the house, I forget exactly how many. Close to a hundred, I think. Would you be interested in the land?"

Meg shook her head. "I can't afford it, Erin. No telling what an acre of land in Wilson County is going for these days. A thousand at least, I'm sure."

"Well, there shouldn't be a problem separating the house from the acreage. Although Heaven knows what will happen to the property when Melody and I are gone. We're the last. Both of us were childless. Though there is a relative on the Kelly side, a younger adopted brother somewhere in Alabama. The land would go to him or to his heirs, I suppose."

"But if the house is auctioned off, someone else could buy it."

Erin smiled. "A silent auction, my dear girl. Virtually unadvertised, the way things are usually done to comply with the letter of the law." The elderly woman struggled to rise from her chair.

Meg jumped up to give her a hand. "It's good of you to see me, Erin. I appreciate your allowing me to come."

"And since you have a long journey ahead, let's go out to the garage and find the box of Lucy's things. I never had much interest in it, though Mother kept a letter Caleb wrote to her after Lucy's disappearance, and of course she'd been sworn to secrecy and couldn't tell him she died. I think she had to suffer from the promise to keep Faith's secret for the rest of her life. It aged her, she said."

They went through a side door off the dining room leading to an attached garage that smelled of mildew. Boxes were neatly arranged on shelves along a back wall.

"Here it is. Earl was such a tidy man, my second husband. When he passed away six years ago, I had to hire a housekeeper to come in twice a week. Being such a fussbudget about organization and cleanliness, Earl spoiled me. If you'd pick this up for me, Meg."

The box clearly marked LUCY had been taped shut. Meg took it from the shelf reverently, as if she were holding a king's ransom. Perhaps the clue she sought resided within.

Though Erin invited her to stay for tea, Meg declined, worried that her visit had already been too much of an intrusion into the frail woman's life. Surely entertaining a complete stranger who appeared at her doorstep was not a regular occurrence for Erin Sumptner.

"I have pets, and I must be home to feed them. My younger daughter took care of them last night, but..."

"Oh, you have children?"

"Two girls, twenty-nine and eighteen. Claire and Jenny."

"How fortunate for you, Meg. If there's anything in the old house you and your daughters would care to have, please do. Otherwise, after you've bought the house, feel at liberty to sell the contents at auction, whatever you deem might be salvageable."

They stood on the front porch of Erin's narrow row-house. Meg held out her left hand. "This was Lucy's. I slipped it on my finger the day I took inventory, and I've been wearing it ever since. It's silly, I know, but it makes me feel close to her memory."

"A lovely ring. Please keep it, if it brings you such pleasure. But don't worry about the house falling into other hands. When we separate out the acreage, no one would want that old white elephant anyhow, other than you."

"Thank you, Erin. Let me know when it goes on the auction block."

"Oh, I shall. So nice to have met you, Meg. Have a safe trip home, now."

On the long drive back, Meg's thoughts were whirling. Almost before she knew it, she pulled off 81 to drive the three miles to the courthouse parking lot to retrieve her car.

Well, now it appeared she'd be the guaranteed owner of the log house, before she was certain she even wanted to be. What had she managed to get herself into this time?

Finally, she drove in the driveway of her own home, parking beside Nell's Escort. Every light in the house was on. Were they having a party? No, no cars. What, then?

"Mom, you're home!" Jenny leaped from the couch to greet her with a hug. "I didn't think you'd ever get here!"

"I'm glad to see you, too," Meg replied with a laugh. Predictably, her three cats were aloof, angry with her for going away. "Did the animals give you any trouble?"

Nell spoke up. "Just hissed all night long. And Cherry barked and wouldn't shut up. Jenny, do you want to tell her, or should I?"

"We don't want you to stay in this house, Mom. Nell and I think it's haunted."

Jenny's earnest expression struck Meg as mildly unsettling. She hadn't imagined the girls would have any strange experiences in her house, or she'd never have asked them to stay overnight.

Casually, she asked, "What makes you think so?"

"Doors closing by themselves," Nell said. "Somebody crying in the middle of the night."

"And when we tried to find out who it was, the crying came from somewhere else. Mom, we were really frightened."

"Well, I'm home now, and if the house really is haunted, I'm here for the duration."

"I *knew* you'd say that," Jenny protested. "Nell, what did I tell you?"

"Why don't you ladies come out to the car and give me a hand? I have a few things to carry in."

As a child, Jenny used to remind her mother of the hope that, when Meg came home from a business trip, she'd brought some little present, and today was no exception.

"Did you bring me a surprise?" Jenny asked, sounding much younger than her years.

"A dozen assorted bagels from the Richmond Bagel Shop, and some special coffee from that little specialty store on Carey Street."

"Cool! Thanks, Mom."

Then the girls were gone, and Meg was alone with the box of Lucy's things. She shoved it into the back of her closet. She refused to allow herself to think about it until she had ample time to browse through the contents.

Besides, this weekend her work was cut out for her, if she planned to draft the report for Marty and ask Joanne to type it first thing Monday morning.

She sighed deeply in the face of such boredom as she removed the burgeoning stack of regulations, exceptions, amendments to the exceptions from her suitcase, leaving the ream of paper on the coffee table in the living room.

She retreated to the bathroom to wash the make-up from her face. To be a public servant in this day and age, with the constantly shifting political developments on the federal, state, and local levels, she'd have had to have been Houdini to remain on top of it all.

Houdini! Caleb had been a magician with a traveling magic show, with Lucy as his assistant, and...

"Meg Kites," she said to her reflection in the bathroom mirror. "Stop it."

Chapter Fourteen

"Talk about suffering here below, and let's keep following Jeee-sus."

Meg hummed along with the gospel tune, sung in an *a cappella* duet of a haunting minor-third harmony, while she assembled the sweet potato casserole for Thanksgiving dinner. The turkey neck, heart, liver, and giblets simmered in a saucepan to be minced for gravy. Last night she'd spent hours making the pies – pumpkin, cranberry-apple, and pecan. The aroma of stuffed turkey from the oven lured the cats into the kitchen.

"The gospel train is coming. Oh, don't you want to go. And leave this world of sorrow, and troubles far below."

Cooking seemed thoroughly enjoyable, her time in the kitchen a vivid contrast to her job of shuffling papers in an existential nightmare with no end. It reminded her of times past, when she and Jack and the girls were a family. Thanksgiving, Christmas, Easter, and birthdays had been festive meal occasions.

Now, after so many years trapped in the kitchen to produce elaborate dinners like clockwork, she had no one to cook for. Her vast collection of cookbooks sat in a cupboard, rarely opened after her separation from Jack.

Hosting Thanksgiving for the girls had been Meg's idea, one way to see Jenny who, between her job and her friends, forgot to check in with her mother on a regular basis.

Planning, shopping, and preparing the meal had consumed some of Meg's idle hours. Jenny and her roommates would be arriving at three o'clock, as they planned to visit with Nell's parents at six.

Since her return from Richmond, she'd successfully resisted

delving into the box of Lucy Hill's papers. She had been out to the old house twice, again with her notepad, this time to estimate what needed to be done to make the house habitable for residents accustomed to twentieth-century conveniences, how much it might cost, and how long she could space the renovations in order to afford them. One thing at a time. But there was no telling when the auction would be, or whether Meg would have the money to buy the old Caleb Hill place.

When Jenny drove up in the Mazda and Nell pulled her Escort in back, the driveway was crammed. Why two cars?

"Hi, Mom. I've missed you." Jenny gave her a hug. "Something smells delicious. Makes my mouth water."

"I made your favorite. Pecan pie."

"Hi, Mrs. Kites," Nell said, also giving her an awkward hug.

"Where's Brianna?" Meg had set the table for four.

"At Joe's grandmother's house. She asked us to convey her apologies for not calling you, but this just came up."

As Meg removed the turkey from the oven and spooned the dressing into an earthenware bowl, a light snow had begun to fall.

"While I'm getting this on the table, why don't you two go look in the log house? The key is in the back of the chimney under a dark-gray stone. It slides out from the chimney. Be sure and replace the key. And take the flashlight."

"You want to, Nell?"

"Sure. Sounds fun."

"Don't be too long. All I have to do yet is make the giblet gravy and steam the Brussels sprouts."

Their timing was perfect, for Meg heard them come through the back door as she was draining the vegetables over the kitchen sink.

"Look what we found. You won't believe this, Mom."

Meg wheeled around to see Jenny holding the gray stone. She pulled the two halves apart to reveal a transparent creature.

"Lord, what is it?"

"See the feet? It's a frog, living in the rock all this time."

"I didn't know such a thing was possible," Meg said, examining the frog more closely. "It's struggling to breathe! Oh, put it outside,

Jenny. Please!"

"It's going to die anyway, Mrs. Kites."

As they bent over the colorless frog, it twitched a few times and was still.

"How did this happen, Jenny? That rock was solid the other day when I replaced it in the chimney."

"It was when we found the key, too. But when we started to put the key back, the rock fell apart in Nell's hand."

Taking a plastic bag from beneath the sink, Meg slipped it over the rock and the ill-fated amphibian and set it on the back porch.

"What are you going to do, Mom? Save it?"

"Hardly. It's another oddity for Ted Rucker, the guy who works upstairs from me. I wouldn't be at all surprised if he thinks I purposely invented this one to get a rise out of him. Which makes more sense than a frog living inside a rock and dying in seconds once it was exposed to the air. He thinks I attract weirdness. But your frog has got to be one for the record books."

"Look what else we found." Jenny handed over a sepia-toned daguerreotype that Meg held under the light of the stove hood.

A photograph of a tall, thin man with dark eyes and hair and mustache. In a black waistcoat.

The hair stood up on Meg's arms. She turned the photograph over and saw, in a woman's spidery penmanship, *Caleb, 1903 – Ian's funeral.*

Softly, she asked, "Where did you find this?"

"On the dining room table," Jenny said.

"But that's impossible! It wasn't there before."

Jenny gave Nell a significant look, not lost on Meg. "See? We told you the place is haunted."

"It really was there, Mrs. Kites. Right by that leaf thing."

"But I distinctly remember. The skeleton leaves were on the side-board."

"Maybe so, Mom. But not today. It was on the table, beside the photograph."

Meg slipped the picture of Caleb Hill into a kitchen drawer. "Time to wash up, and time to eat, ladies."

"The snow's really coming down out there, Mom. Have you heard the weather report?"

"This morning they were calling for rain. I guess the cold front passing through is colder than they thought."

Meg lit the candles while Nell and Jenny rinsed their hands at the sink. When they sat down to share the meal, it was four o'clock. An hour later, two inches of snow covered the ground.

"Oh, great!" Jenny said, opening the front door and stepping out to the porch. "Boy, am I glad I don't have to work tonight."

"I'm going to call my mother and tell her we can't come." Nell picked up the phone.

"Mom, we have to leave. The back roads may get worse."

"And then you'll be stranded, Jenny. Why don't the two of you stay here tonight? I'm off tomorrow. If you need help, I'll be around."

"That's okay, Mom. We turned the furnace down to save energy, and if it gets really cold tonight, the pipes could freeze. So we have to be at the trailer."

"Well, here. Let me wrap up some of the leftovers."

Meg watched from the door as Nell drove down the blacktop road with Jenny in the rear. She had made them promise to call her when they got home.

Listlessly, she poked at her slice of pumpkin pie. She set down the fork, turned on the television to the local news, and removed Caleb Hill's photograph from the drawer, a photograph taken on the day he and Lucy buried their infant son.

She studied his eyes, and they seemed so vibrant and full of life that she almost felt as though he stared back at her. She propped the photo against the candlestick and continued to regard Caleb Hill as she finished her pie. He had been an exceedingly handsome man.

Midway through the weather report, Jenny called to let her mother know they'd made it safely to the trailer.

"Yes, and you'll not be able to leave," Meg warned. "We're supposed to get up to a foot of snow over the next two days. *Then* what, young lady?"

"We have friends with four-wheel drives and chains for their tires. Oh, and thanks for the food, Mom. Our frig was nearly empty. But please don't worry about me. We'll be okay."

Easier said than done. Meg still found herself fretting over Claire, and she was twenty-nine years of age. Oh, well. If Jenny needed her, Meg knew she would call.

When she got up in the middle of the night to make a turkey sandwich, she looked outside. The snow came down in buckets.

She ate the sandwich, surveying the remaining leftovers in the refrigerator. She and the cats wouldn't have to worry about what to eat this weekend

Chapter Fifteen

At daybreak, Meg woke up anticipating three days alone in the house with her animals, no deadlines to meet, no run-ins with the likes of Mr. Feder, snug and safe as the snow continued to fall. If only she could have kept herself from worrying over Jenny, it might have been a perfect respite, one that was long overdue. She hadn't been able to take a real vacation in more than seven years.

It was a treat just to wear her flannel nightgown all morning. She drank her coffee and listened to the local radio station repeat the weather report every fifteen minutes, suspecting the local store shelves were emptied of bread, milk, and eggs. Whenever the slightest hint of foul weather threatened, the rural residents bought out the basic necessities.

She gazed at the photograph of Caleb Hill, a flesh-and-blood man rather than a disembodied figment of her own imagination, and took solace in this evidence that she wasn't menopausal looney-tunes, after all.

His expression was stern, but not sad. Peculiar, when he had just buried his son. But Lucy might have done the mourning for both. Perhaps Caleb Hill was a rare man whose wife had been able to lean on him for strength.

Meg could see why Lucy had fallen in love. The longer she studied his likeness, the more she wanted to learn about Caleb and the details of the life he'd shared with his sunny Irish wife.

Irresistibly drawn to Lucy's box, Meg fetched it from the closet and cut the tape with a kitchen knife. She carried the box into the living room to place on the coffee table, hefted the welfare regulations to the piano bench, and sat down on the couch.

Already, she felt guilty. Marty wanted addendum information, thanks to questions at the Board of Supervisors meeting about how many recipients would be exempt from Workfare, and why. She'd meant to plow through the conference materials again, compose a bulleted list of exceptions, and be done with it. But the box seemed to beckon to her. She rationalized that it wouldn't hurt to take a peek or two, not after it had been sitting in her closet like a wonderful secret she couldn't wait to plumb for three weeks.

Unfolding the flaps, she released a musty odor from a box kept in storage for decades, and momentarily she was almost afraid of what she might find.

Lucy's Bible with a worn, black-leather cover. She opened the first few pages to that scent peculiar to Bibles and read the dates of birth for Melody Catherine Hill and Ian Caleb Hill. Throughout the Bible, favorite scriptures had been neatly marked with a thin black line, Lucy, the minister's daughter.

Tucked inside the back cover was a letter addressed to Catherine Kelly Bishop in Richmond. Meg removed the onion skin pages from the envelope.

April, 1905

Dear Catherine:

She was the most beautiful girl in Wilson County, and I didn't give a fig what Lucas or his wife thought of her. Lucy was my only choice for a bride.

My brother moves in different circles of society. As a respected barrister, Lucas Hill conducts business with all classes of citizens. Faith is a good wife for Lucas, but she tends to judge folks severely, and I cannot forget how she expressed her extreme displeasure about her brother-in-law's interest in Lucinda Kelly, the girl she called nothing but an Irish immigrant hired as Faith's live-in domestic.

I had been away for four months with the Southline Railroad, as far as California that time. The only home I claimed were rooms over a shop on the main street of town. Yes, at twenty-seven years of age, I lived alone in two rooms above Robbin's Apothecary.

There had been one woman at the University of Virginia, but she eloped with a Northerner. Caleb Hill wasn't one to render much challenge, for I did not truly love her. I believe Lucas had begun to despair that I would marry, destined to remain a bachelor forever. But when I returned to Wilson and saw her for the first time, I was helpless before the sparkle in her eyes, her wit, and her great beauty. She was so alive!

All my life, I capitulated to Lucas in most things, particularly after our parents died, first Papa and then Mother. I went off to the university and studied Commerce, despite my great desire to become an illusionist. Lucas enjoyed a hearty laugh over that profitless ambition. He said no brother of his would bring disgrace on the Hill name by waving a magic baton like a simple-minded charlatan.

Dear Catherine, I have taken the liberty of writing to you to inquire about letters from Lucy you may have in your possession which speak of our life together. I would be forever in your debt should you send them to me. I fear I cannot live without her. Until I find her, reading her thoughts in her own hand would give me no small measure of comfort and a sense that she is still near.

And one thing more. Picture me on my knees begging you to reveal when you hear from Lucy. As you know, she has not been well since the son died. And now with this pregnancy, this infant she does not seem to welcome, I fear for her very life, even for her immortal soul.

Please, do not doubt my love for your sister Lucy. I implore you, Catherine. Should you learn of her whereabouts, I must be the first to know. I will travel to the ends of the earth to bring her home with me. Your brother by marriage,

With most sincere regards,

Caleb Hill

Tears stung Meg's eyes. She folded the letter and replaced it in the Bible.

Lucy had been pregnant for a third time when she died. For suddenly Meg had little doubt that Lucy had taken her own life.

With this tangible proof of Caleb's deep love for his wife, for the first time Meg began to understand the deception invented by Lucas and Faith. Perhaps they feared that, with no hope that Lucy was still alive, Caleb might have died by his own hand. And if he'd suspected she'd killed herself, if in any way he had held himself responsible, it would have been unendurable.

There were no letters from Lucy to Catherine here, so Catherine must have kept them for herself. Unless she had honored Caleb's request and sent Lucy's letters to him.

Christmas cards, a photograph of a smiling, carefree Lucy posed on the same bicycle now in the bedroom of the old log house. Several yellowed recipes clipped from magazines: sweet potato pie, prune and port compote, fried apple pies, sardine spread.

On the bottom of the box was a book whose cover said *Gardening Journal*, an antique version of a printed book one might buy today in a stationery store. The pages were decorated with drawings of fruits and vegetables, ladles and jars. It was Lucy's book, but she hadn't used it merely to jot down her garden output. Here, she had recorded her thoughts.

June 3, 1897. Today I become Mrs. Caleb Hill. Catherine shipped the brown dress from Richmond. My bouquet of gardenias and orange blossoms has arrived by rail from Roanoke. We shall honeymoon in White Sulphur Springs at a resort Caleb has visited. I vow to make him a good wife.

Ours is a small house, but in the country as I wished. I despise the concerns of polite society. Dull women coming to call is a dreadful waste of one's time. I have no patience for it. I cherish a life with Caleb, removed from judgmental eyes such as those of my prying sister-in-law. Here, we shall have our privacy.

Several pages were left blank. Meg kept turning.

March 17, 1898. Caleb has given me the velvet divan I admired from the catalogue. He had it shipped by rail from Boston. I do so wish he were not away from home so often. When he performs his magic show, I will see even less of him unless I may go, as well. But I have encouraged him to follow his dream.

December 31, 1900. This has been a wonderful year. Our daughter Melody was born, and we take such delight in her. Caleb has become a member of the American Society for Psychical Research.

Caleb is forever bringing me presents. I ask him not to, but he says it pleases him to see me smile. I love him so.

July 1902. We have done such a great deal of travel with Caleb's magic show. I assist him on stage. We are now in Kansas City. Melody is with Faith and Lucas.

Faith would have been a good mother, had Providence seen fit to give her a child of her own. Faith tells me a mother's place is with her child. Though she tries to cover it, I know she disapproves of me, still. She always has.

October 3, 1903. We buried baby Ian in the cemetery today. Caleb worries for me. I try not to weep.

In between, there were snippets, remarks about the weather, how many jars of string-beans she had put up, notes on altering a dress pattern. The last ten or twelve pages had been torn from the book. Meg felt cheated. How she wished there had been more to read.

She got up, packing all but the gardening book and the photograph of Lucy on the bicycle into the box. She propped the picture beside Caleb's, wondering why she had developed such a fascination for this couple and their past lives. Perhaps Meg had missed her calling, and she'd have been happier as a historian or archivist rather than a social services director.

The snow had not abated, and she had no desire to walk outside to measure its depth. It was enough to see the cats take mincing steps on the snow, only to dash back into the house with wet paws that left prints on the linoleum. A dozen times she started to dial Jenny's number, but forced herself not to. She spent the rest of the day compiling the report for Marty, her mind numbed from the chore.

For lack of a program to watch on television or a new novel from the library to read, Meg went to bed early. The wind had come up, a howling wind blowing snow into drifts. She had to climb from her warm bed to latch the storm door when the wind banged it repeatedly against the side of the house.

Restless, assailed by strange dreams, she kept waking during the night to mark the snow's progress. Pounding on her pillow and trying to find a comfortable place for her head, Meg thought of Lucy Hill. If the pages hadn't been ripped from the book, she might have learned something of Lucy's final days.

Had Lucy committed suicide as a result of post-partum depression, the local clergy refusing to perform the last Christian rites and bury her in hallowed ground? But then again, if she hadn't died but had really disappeared...

Nudged from an uneasy sleep, Meg was instantly wakeful. At first she thought it was the wind, but then she recognized the sound of a woman weeping, a high keening carried by the wind, a wailing from the very depths of human misery. As she held her breath and continued to listen, she heard someone call to her.

Mary Margaret!

Maa-ry Maah-gret!

But how could that be? No one had called her Mary Margaret since her mother passed away.

The wind died down instantly. She'd have thought she had dreamed it, were it not for the fact that, at three a.m., she was wide awake. Tossing and turning, eventually she managed to doze off sometime before daylight.

And in the morning, an odd smell filled the house, the fragrance of summer flowers. Impossible, of course, but there, nonetheless – an unmistakable scent of lilacs. She looked out at the winter scene. The snow had stopped falling.

Meg put on a jacket, gloves, and rubber boots and took the broom to the back porch to clear a path down the basement stairs. With the weight of the snow on tree limbs, there might be a power outage, and at some point Meg would need to check the basement fuse box. The frigid air froze her nostrils and burned her chest when she sucked it into her lungs.

She returned to the kitchen for the pies wrapped in tin foil to store in the basement freezer, to remove temptation. Painstakingly, by counting calories and fat grams, she'd managed to lose six pounds. She didn't get nearly enough exercise, her major problem, and had resolved to join a fitness center in the spring.

Clomping out to the shed for the snow shovel, she stepped in snow that came almost to her knees. She had to kick the drifts away from the door of the shed to open it. With the shovel, she spent an hour making pathways to the house and clearing the front sidewalk. By the time she finished, she was exhausted. In the house, the phone rang, and she hurried to answer.

"Mom, are you all right? I had dreams about you being hurt. I can't remember what they were."

"I'm okay. I'm just back in from shoveling the walks. Lord, I didn't realize I was so out of shape. It's embarrassing. How are you faring out there?"

"As you said, we're snowed in, but we're waiting on a farmer to plow out our road to the highway."

"And what will it cost, Jenny?"

"Twenty dollars," she answered with a groan. "But I have to get to work tomorrow. They already called me to make sure I'll be in."

"What's your shift?"

"Eight until six, the busiest and longest."

"I'll come through for breakfast and say hey, if they plow my road."

"Promise me you won't do anything else strenuous, Mom. What if you had a heart attack? You'd be all alone."

"To tell the truth, I hadn't thought of that. You're right. I'll cool it."

She heated a cup of coffee in the microwave and sat down at the kitchen table with her notes. She was amassing quite a mess, between clues from Faith Hill's missives in the shoeboxes from the attic, information from Dr. Mitchum, scribblings resulting from her visit with Erin Sumptner in Richmond, and Lucy's own words from her journal.

She read through the sketchy entries in Lucy's hand. Meg hadn't expected to discover a diary describing the events of everyday life in minute detail and, really, she felt blessed in having even a few of Lucy's thoughts. Now she was compelled to put it all together, to try and discern a pattern. Then she might see the gaps, to find out what vital bits of information were missing and might never be found. On a fresh sheet of paper, she wrote:

Year	Event	Source(s)
1869	Caleb born	Bureau of Vital Stat.
1875 (est.)	Lucy born	Erin Sumptner
1897	Marriage	Lucy's journal
1897	Faith against	Faith's papers
1897	Lucy's Christmas card to Lucas/Faith	
1900	Melody born	
	Caleb joins ASPR	Lucy's journal
1902	Magic show	"
1903	Ian stillborn	"
1905	Lucy pregnant	Caleb's letter
	Dies (disappears?)	
1916	Caleb's memorial service;	
	Log house sealed	Faith's papers
1962	Faith 'haunted'; dies.	

Those were the only events for which she had a date and one or more sources. When the roads were cleared of snow, she thought of returning to the courthouse for documented evidence of their marriage, and to learn whether Lucas or Faith had filed a death certificate for Lucy that might not have found its way to Richmond.

Or a death certificate for Caleb. Lucas was an attorney, and having Melody's parents legally declared dead would have been a sure way for Lucas and Faith to retain permanent custody of their niece.

For several hours, Meg tried to occupy herself with knitting, writing a letter to Claire and one to Chris, washing a few sweaters by hand and laying them out to dry. Later Jenny called to say their road was scraped, and Nell had made a snack-food run into town.

Another turkey sandwich for dinner, and Meg got ready for bed and climbed beneath the covers to re-read *Of Human Bondage*, one of her favorite novels moved from house to house over the years. Visualizing Bette Davis in the star role, Meg fell asleep mid-chapter, neglecting to turn off the bedside light.

There was a dream of an infant mewling, hidden in tall grass. Meg searched in the weeds, listening for the direction of the crying. Ecstatic, she bent down to pick up the naked child.

The infant's hands were covered with blood.

"Mary Margaret!"

Someone punched her on the arm, hard, and pulled her hair. In the dream Meg struggled to escape her antagonist, then felt a sharp bite on her leg and heard more than felt the resounding crack of a slap across her face.

She awoke all at once and sat up in bed, as an unseen presence tried to push her to the floor. When she resisted, abruptly the pressure on her left side stopped. She flipped back the covers and looked at her thigh: a distinct impression of teeth marks.

Why would anyone direct violence against Meg Kites? Unless her inquiries about members of the Hill family were not welcomed.

Then she realized that not one of her cats slept on her bed. She got up to find them stretched out in the living room, Cappy beneath the piano bench and close to a warm vent, Sweet Babu draped across the back of the sofa, and Bart curled up in a chair. Cherry Lamb snuffled and snored in a corner of the couch.

Meg went to the bathroom to put alcohol on her thigh, but the mark had disappeared, as though she'd only dreamed it.

Climbing into bed, she said, "Whoever you are, I mean you no harm. Just leave me the hell alone, so I can get some sleep. Or else!"

At dawn Bart came to wake her, to a cold house filled not with the fragrance of lilacs but with the sour smell of oil. She turned up the thermostat in the living room: nothing.

She felt like kicking herself for not calling a service man at the first sign of trouble. *Now* what? Where would she find someone to come on a Sunday, and on a holiday weekend, to boot?

Suddenly the idea of buying a wood stove as a back-up heat source didn't seem quite so frivolous. Here she was, trapped at home on a Sunday with no heat.

Had the ghostly presence decided to freeze her out of her own home? Well, in a pig's eye!

Meg dressed and went down to the basement to carry two space heaters upstairs. She plugged in both heaters, one in the living room and one in the kitchen. Then she decided to go for broke, turned on the oven and left the door open. She brewed coffee and sat in the kitchen, perfectly warm for the moment, reading her novel through the long hours and finishing it just before nightfall.

Then one of the space heaters went into the bathroom, and one in her bedroom. At least she still had hot water and electricity. She told herself it could have been worse.

But the truth was, and she was past fooling herself, she despaired of the prospect of living alone for the rest of her life. If only she could find a contemporary man with the wit and devotion of a Caleb Hill...

But he was dead. Wasn't he? Of course he was. Even if his funeral had been staged because he, too, had disappeared, wherever he had gone, he'd have died long ago.

Then why did Meg feel as though his presence had grown stronger in her mind, as if the vague shapes of memory had begun to coalesce into...

Where do memories go? When the human heart ceases to beat, when the brain no longer functions, what becomes of a man's thoughts and hopes and dreams? And what happens to a love so enduring, so strong, when the lover is no more?

She would probably never know, not from personal experience. Once she had been in love with Jack and, though he'd given her ample reason even from the first months of their marriage, it had taken twenty-five years to finally stop loving him and break free.

Then she'd thought she loved Warren, but with his self-destructive behavior, she began to pity him. And she was not sorry when he died, because he had wanted to die, his death releasing her from the terrible burden of having to be the one to say goodbye.

Warren had believed in nothing but himself, and look where that had gotten him. Sometimes, as she tried to release the day's concerns and fall asleep at night, she remembered how cold and flaccid his hand had felt fifteen minutes after dying. The man with no faith had relinquished his dreams long before, so that when he died he took nothing with him.

Not even Meg's love.

Chapter Sixteen

Joanne, the long-suffering receptionist for the County Department of Social Services, patched through Christmas carols scheduled to play nonstop on the intercom for the next month.

"Mrs. Kites, Ted Rucker returning your call, line seven."

"Thanks, Joanne." Hesitantly, Meg asked a very upset Fran Giddings, the eligibility supervisor, to please excuse her, and punched into Ted's call.

"Meg, what's up? How's tricks in the Land of Nod? Have you hung out your shingle to be Wilson County's official channeler?"

"I'm almost beginning to think I should. Will you be in your office for a while this morning? I have something to show you, and it's a dilly."

"What've you got?"

"A colorless frog completely entombed in a stone that suddenly broke in half of its own accord."

A brief pause. In a less breezy tone, he said, "You're kidding."

"I'll run up and show you."

"I've gotta look for something in my files. Seems to me I remember...well, we'll chat when you get here. I wouldn't miss this for the world, believe me."

"Thanks, Ted. See you in a few."

Meg turned back to Fran who hovered half in and half out the door. "Fran, are you going to suspend Mavis, or shall I?"

Fran sighed. "No, I'll do it, damn it. It makes me so angry she'd put me through this grief!" Fran was too soft-hearted for her own good, and under her lackluster supervision the Mavises of the world tended to get away with murder.

"A week without pay, and maybe she'll think twice about leaving early and signing out for fake appointments. You'll have to keep tabs on her from here on, Fran. You realize."

"Yeah, boss. I read you loud and clear." Then she left with a flare of courage, to get the dirty deed done before she lost her nerve.

Meg wished all her staff were as dedicated and honest as Fran Giddings. She suspected that Mavis wasn't the sole offender, only the most blatant. Every once in a while, as she had reminded Fran, to prevent a mutiny, there has to be a sacrificial lamb.

Joanne's voice, on the intercom again.

"Mrs. Kites, Marty's on line two, and he's fuming."

So, what else was new?

"Joanne, I'll take the call, and then I have to visit with Ted Rucker for a bit. I'll be back afterward, so hold my calls." She took a minute to collect her thoughts. It couldn't have been about the addendum information placed on his desk an hour ago; she knew it was spot-on.

"Good morning, Marty."

"Good morning, my sweet ass! Have you seen the paper?"

"Not yet. I'm on my way out, but I'll..."

"Oh, there's no rush," he said, his words dripping with sarcasm. "Just whenever you find a spare minute, I'd like to hear your views about the article on page three."

"I'll call you." She hung up, grabbed the plastic bag, and hurried upstairs.

Whatever it was, Marty could wait a few minutes. He was accustomed to telling Meg to jump and, faithful Saint Bernard that she was, expecting her to ask in which direction and how high.

Ted Rucker wore his familiar attire – flannel shirt, dungarees, and cowboy boots. He gave every appearance of assuming his doubting Thomas mode. She wasn't surprised to hear him say, "This better be legit, Meg."

"Would I kid an old kidder?"

Carefully, she removed the rock from the plastic and set it on his desk. The frog was still there; she'd checked to verify that it hadn't mysteriously dissolved like the star-jelly vanishing overnight while safely ensconced in her refrigerator.

Before he examined the rock, he asked, "So how are you doing otherwise?"

Meg glanced up at Ted and assessed his expression as one of genuine concern. "Other than being tired of snow, I'm fine. Glad to be back at work, actually, something I didn't think I'd ever say. Four days off, snowbound in my house with my furnace on the blink, was too much for me. Why?"

"Have you had any other strange phenomena?"

"Other than my furnace conking out?"

"No, I meant paranormal stuff."

She considered mentioning the nocturnal wailing, the vivid dream about being attacked in her bed, the ghostly manifestation of the man she took for Caleb Hill floating across the meadow by moonlight. No, better not. This grotesque frog was bizarre enough for one day.

"You want more, Ted? What do you think *this* means?"

"I don't want to freak you out, but I looked it up. The Buddhists think that a state or plane we describe as Hell sometimes happens in our own reality. And a living creature found in solid rock is regarded as a signal of the event. Let's face it, Meg. Such a thing isn't your ordinary, everyday occurrence."

"But haven't you ever heard of similar incidents?"

"Heard of, never saw with my own eyes. Until this minute. Can I keep it?"

"Sure, I suppose. What are you going to do with it?"

"Consult someone in the philosophy department who specializes in Eastern thought, for starters. If I find out anything other than what I just told you, I'll call."

"Well, you're welcome to it. I'd only throw it away, or give the poor little guy a decent burial."

Ted reached for the morning edition of the Roanoke newspaper. "There's an article in here about a visiting British professor who's at the university this semester, a Dr. Hollings, evidently a world-renown parapsychologist. You might consider giving him a call." He handed the paper to her and she began to skim the first few paragraphs of the article. "You know, sort of a professional ghost-hunter. If you talk with him, tell him what we said about ley lines and stuff. Mention the boiling Clorox and the skyfall. And this." Gingerly, he touched the two halves of the stone, the pale frog fallen to the desk blotter on Ted's desk. "This sure beats the hell out of another two-headed calf."

"Maybe I will, Ted. It couldn't hurt, if he can spare me some time." Meg started to hand the newspaper back to him when her eyes caught the headlines of another article on the same page. She read the first two sentences. "Oh, my God! No wonder Marty wants to talk with me. One of my staff members is being held at the county jail."

"No way! One of your staff? Really?"

"I have to call Marty right back. I'll see you, Ted, and thanks."

She ran downstairs to her office, accepting a message slip from Joanne on her way. Good; the furnace repairman was on his way to her house. She had left the doors unlocked and a note on the kitchen table describing Sunday's furnace symptoms, asking the man to call her at the office with a cost estimate of parts and labor to have it fixed. Well, one worry had been taken off her mind.

She dialed Marty's extension. "Marty, I just saw the paper. What were the charges?"

"I've talked with the Sheriff. It seems he was picked up for assault and battery while trying to make a citizen's arrest of a suspected shoplifter in the Walmart parking lot. On his time off, thank God for small favors, not in his official capacity as the county welfare fraud investigator. Which, incidentally, he no longer is. I'm firing the fruitcake, soon as somebody posts bond on his butt."

"You'll have a lawsuit on your hands, Marty. Mark my words. Mr. Feder isn't going to roll over and play dead."

"Who gives a crap? I'm tired of feeling terrorized by Mr. Feder. Fill out his termination papers and have them on my desk by five o'clock. I'm going to run this by the county attorney first, of course."

To her consternation, Meg actually felt a pang of compassion for Norman Feder. As she struggled to force herself to ask whether they might give the man a second chance, Marty hung up. Decision made.

Her words to Fran came back to taunt her. Mr. Feder was today's sacrificial lamb, never mind that from his excessive compulsion to catch the culprits, he'd managed to bring this on himself. Mr. Feder's fate was out of Meg's hands.

She was grateful to be back in the real world, despite her worry about the follow-up article in tomorrow's paper identifying Norman Feder as a county employee. This was just the sort of juicy morsel a cub reporter couldn't wait to see in print. And Marty would go through the ceiling. Wait until the Board of Supervisors heard about this.

She opened her purse and removed the photograph of Caleb Hill, realizing how Jenny's discovery had affected her nascent resolve to end the excursions into the history of the log house.

Looking at his eyes, Meg knew she'd become obsessed. Whatever had occurred in the past life of Caleb Hill was no longer academic, because it had happened to a real person. And to Meg, Caleb's past search had become her present search, as if somehow he had managed to involve her in a quest to solve a dark mystery that had withstood the test of time.

She stared at the image of his face. "What do you want? Why can't you leave me alone?" At the cemetery, she had made a promise to his grave, a promise she now regretted. Meg remembered the dreams she had suffered as a child, the terror of being sensitively attuned to extrasensory perceptions. She'd been deeply frightened then, but now she was an adult, with a rational mind. For one last time, if she could open herself...

The man called about the furnace. The oil feedline was clogged. Thirty dollar service charge. Tonight she'd go home to a warm house.

Meg handled a few minor personnel issues, finished the paperwork on Mr. Feder for Marty, and lunched on yogurt and a banana at her desk. Midway through the afternoon, she went to the lobby and asked Joanne for today's paper. After reading the article featuring Mr. Feder, she turned to the interview of the British parapsychologist.

She found herself picking up the telephone almost as if she had no choice in the matter. Andrew Hollings cheerfully accepted her call and suggested lunch on Tuesday at the faculty restaurant on campus.

"Jot down as much detail as you can, Meg. It will help me to have it as we talk."

"You're referring to paranormal experiences?"

"Whatever you've perceived even a touch out of the ordinary.

Intervals between events would also be of value."

"Well, I don't know if I can remember, not exactly."

"Estimates, then. Do your best. See you tomorrow at noon."

"Thank you, Dr. Hollings."

"Andrew, please. I'm looking forward to it."

That night at home, perversely, nothing unusual happened. But Meg wrote down anything she could recall. The ghost of the man on the road. The wispy shape on the porch of the old house that had conveyed a feminine feeling.

The boiling solution in the bucket.
The dark cloud and the meteor. Star-jelly the next morning.
A recurring sound of weeping.
The bite on her thigh.
Meg's cats and their skittish behavior, the dog barking at thin air.
The smell of lilacs in her house.
What had she forgotten? Oh, yes. The frog in the stone.

Reviewing the list before tucking it in her purse, Meg thought that, if Dr. Hollings didn't take her for a lunatic, these signs should give him plenty to decipher.

The next morning when she got to the office, Fran Giddings hit Meg for a donation to add to the kitty for bailing Mr. Feder out of jail.

"I don't know how I could have been so callous, Fran. It didn't once dawn on me about Norm not having anyone else. I feel like an ingrate, knowing he had to spend two nights in jail. How much do we need to spring him?"

"Seventy-five dollars. A tenth of his bond."

"How much do you have?"

"Twenty-seven dollars. And getting that much out of the staff was like picking hen's teeth."

"I'll make up the difference." Meg wrote a check to Fran Giddings, asking her to cash it at the credit union.

"You can kiss this goodbye, Meg. You know darned well he'll never pay us back."

"Consider it guilt money. Don't worry about it."

"Say, you look spiffy today," Fran said. "Important meeting?"

"Lunch at the university."

"Well, cherry-red's a good color on you. You should wear it more often. Listen, I'll go ahead and take care of Feder's bail. Then I'll be back."

"Godspeed on your mission of mercy," Meg replied, fanning her out the door. She tried not to think of Norman Feder tossed into the middle of the general jail population, at the hands of *wastrels*. She only hoped the jailors had closeted the poor man in his own cell.

Chapter Seventeen

Meg had chosen her best red-wool suit with a black shell and gold jewelry, trying to impress Dr. Hollings as anything but a kook. But then again, perhaps most of the people he met in his special line of work as professional ghost-hunter *were* kooks.

At eleven-forty-five, she parked in the visitors section of the lot adjacent to the university conference center and crossed the street that led to the building, veering to the right for the faculty dining room.

A short, rotund, bespectacled man in a tweed blazer with leather patches on the sleeves waited at the register and introduced himself as Andrew Hollings. He had a shiny bald pate and a shaggy fringe of gray hair girdling his round head. He had reserved a table for two. Gallantly, he touched her elbow lightly as he guided her to the table.

Seating herself, Meg tried to think of an opening remark. "And what brings you to Virginia?"

"Why, didn't you know? Virginia's credited with more resident ghosts than any other state. Yes, the Commonwealth is quite rich in ghosts, goblins, and things going bump in the night." He chuckled, his blue eyes merry behind his bifocals.

After they ordered lunch, Meg handed over her list.

"Interesting!" Dr. Hollings peered through the bottom of his eyeglasses. "Seems you've experienced a veritable spate of paranormal events. How long did you say you've lived in the house?"

"Six months. The past two months have been the active period. Absolutely nothing unusual during the first four, at least not that I noticed."

"Perhaps the spirit was testing you, Meg."

She took a sip of iced water. "Dr. Hollings, do you actually believe in spirits?"

"Oh my yes. Yes, I do. Why, don't you?"

"I'm afraid to answer in the affirmative. I've been resisting a yes answer. But now I think I may be beyond that point. Actually, I'd like to know whether my perceptions are real and my feelings emanate from something truly...*there*, and aren't just my own over-active imagination."

A young waitress brought their chef salads with Dr. Hollings' side order of cornbread and pinto beans. "I do enjoy your Southern cuisine," he said, digging into the beans crusted with sweet relish and chopped onions.

With a quirk of her eyebrow and a light tone of voice, Meg said, "How strange, to be having lunch with a British scholar who believes in the existence of ghosts."

"I'm not alone, I can assure you. There's an entire body of knowledge developed over the years. It really began to catch fire in the United Kingdom toward the middle of the last century. Such spiritualists as Daniel Dunglas Home, who died in 1886 at the age of 53, having astounded people with his levitation and other feats."

Meg let her fork fall to the plate, feeling as if she were in a lecture hall. Her attention was riveted to Dr. Hollings, who took mincing bites of his salad and continued his discourse.

"But spiritualism had its real resurgence after World War One, when wives and mothers and a father or two were desperate to contact the spirits of their young men killed in battle. You may be sure, there were many spiritualists adept at fakery, convincing to patrons anxious to believe and quite willing to pay handsomely for the privilege. And you have conducted a bit of research into your ghost?"

Sheepishly, Meg admitted she had. "I believe his name is Caleb Hill, and he's searching for his wife, Lucy."

"We call it veridical hallucination, when later research verifies that what you have seen in the apparition represents an actual person in terms of his appearance, his life, and so forth. Tell me, did Lucy die a violent death?"

"I'm not sure. One source suggests she disappeared, another that she committed suicide and was buried in an unmarked grave."

"What do you feel your ghost is trying to communicate?"

"I don't know."

With gusto, Dr. Hollings returned to his pinto beans and corn-bread. "Why don't you ask him?"

She responded with a nervous laugh. "You're teasing, aren't you?"

"No, no, my dear. Quite the contrary. You may be residing on a highly-energized site. If you have natural psychic ability, this could result in an increase in telepathy, visions, automatic writing, even retrocognition."

"Retrocognition?"

"When you might experience firsthand the events from the past. Rare, but possible. Highly possible."

"But how could that be, Dr. Hollings?"

He used his napkin to dab at his lips. "To understand the theory, you must entertain the possibility of other dimensions existing apart from our own. There's the time-warp theory, another dimension bleeding into our own, a dimension of which most of us are totally ignorant. Retrocognition, or time-slips, can be explained as moments when the past and present collide. Some feel there is a reality called the Other Now, an alternative universe parallel to our own, and we are ever in danger of being sucked into the Other Now, right over the barrier between the two universes. You could consider a ghost or spirit to be a life-print in time, much like a footprint in sand."

"If there's truth to any of this, how could I begin to communicate with a ghost?"

"Through a medium. I can furnish you the name of an exceptionally good medium I've met with a number of times since arriving in Virginia, primarily to verify certain facts about departed spirits from the Appalachians purportedly related to the Civil War. Here." He jotted down a name and phone number on the back of his business card and gave it to Meg. "But if you're uncomfortable consulting a medium, you could try the Ouija board. You simply ask a specific question and wait until your ghost responds. If she or he is in the mood, that is."

A nagging fear began to envelop her. "But aren't Ouija boards supposed to be dangerous?"

Dr. Hollings treated himself to an indulgent chuckle. "The American movies have given the old Ouija a bad press, I'm afraid. But not to gloss over, the truth is we're speaking of a dangerous subject, ghosts. If you had given me the slightest indication that this ghost of yours was anything but harmless and benign...he doesn't frighten you, apparently."

"No, but..."

"Then the Ouija could be a good way to connect. Worth a try, certainly."

Meg watched as the parapsychologist polished off the last of the pinto beans by stabbing a row of beans with the tines of his fork, then sopping up the bean liquor with cornbread.

"Dr. Hollings, I was raised Catholic, and my parish priest told me to shun things of the occult. Part of my hesitation is due to my upbringing, I guess."

"Well, who do you suppose performs exorcisms? The Catholics. Always have. So they know whereof they speak. Please, don't take my suggestions literally, if they run counter to your deepest beliefs. I wouldn't want you to, Meg, not in any case."

Meg admired the man's flexible attitude. "But do you really believe we can contact the dead?"

Andrew Hollings smiled at her, setting down his fork. "Let me tell you a story. You've heard, of course, of Harry Houdini. There were two women in Harry's life, his mother and his wife, Bess. When Houdini's mother died, he spent years attending countless séances in search of a message from his mother. He was furious when the spiritualists he consulted regurgitated animal tissue for ectoplasm, or vomited cheesecloth and called it the manifestation of a spirit. He declared spiritualism a terrible fraud, a hoax perpetrated by charlatans. He then made a death pact with his wife Bess. They agreed that the first to die would contact the surviving spouse. Well, Houdini died before Bess, in 1926."

"What happened?"

Dr. Hollings smiled again, his fingers clasped beneath his double chin, his blue eyes glistening. "When Bess attended a séance with the famous medium Arthur Ford, a message came through, Harry's secret code with Bess, the jumbled words of an old vaudeville song, 'Rosabelle,

I love you more than I can tell.' Instantly, Bess believed, only to later remember that Harry's secret code was published a year following his death. And in subsequent séances, Harry never contacted Bess again."

"So you're telling me it's *not* possible."

"I'm simply suggesting it's only probable if one believes. You must be truly receptive, or no communication is likely. But again, some should never attempt it, for various personal reasons of their own. I call it a psychic safety valve, so the spirits can only get through to conduits open to them." Dr. Hollings glanced at his watch. "Well, I must be going, Meg. Our meeting has been delightful. I do wish you the very best of luck, in the pursuit of your ghost."

Meg thanked him for his time. Her mind was whirling.

"Oh, one last thing, my dear. As a Catholic, it may give you comfort. St. Francis de Sales said, 'Make yourself familiar with the angels, and behold them frequently in spirit; for without being seen, they are present with you.'"

She stood up and walked with him to the register, where he insisted on taking her check. They shook hands. Walking to her car, she realized that Dr. Hollings had kept the list she had prepared for him. Perhaps he would include her story in a scholarly treatise for publication, on his paranormal experiences in Virginia.

On route to her office, she swung down Depot Street to Cambria and parked in front of an antique and curio shop. An ornate Ouija board sat in the front window. She asked the proprietor its price, and for fifty dollars, she became the dubious owner of an antique Ouija board.

She could have purchased a new Milton-Bradley version at K-Mart, and probably for less. But if she intended to try and talk with Caleb, it seemed appropriate that the vehicle of communication should have once belonged to his own era.

Meg placed the board and its planchette in the hatch of her car and returned to the office, to finish out the day.

****

As if preparing for a white Christmas, December blew intermittent blasts of snow on an almost daily basis. An anemic sun might appear from behind the clouds for a few hours, only to be swallowed by storms whose persistence seemed almost vengeful.

The old-timers around Wilson County warned over the morning radio station about the Farmer's Almanac calling for a winter precipitation total of two hundred inches, worse than last winter. The jocular announcer reminded the listening audience that an inch of rain, when the temperature was below freezing, equaled a foot of snow.

With the old log house bundled in snowdrifts, Meg had not been in the mood to brave the elements even the short distance from her house to the Hill place. The door was locked, the windows were secure, and the key hung on Meg's key holder in the kitchen.

For days she'd wrestled with herself, arguing the point of whether or not she should dabble in what Father Cavanaugh had called the occult. She studied the brief chronology she'd developed, convinced that if she thought about it long enough, an essential clue that had previously eluded her would surface in her mind.

But there was more to her obsession for communicating with departed spirits than Caleb Hill. Meg had a more personal reason, for she had never had the chance to say she was sorry to her own mother before she died.

After a terrible argument over Jenny's outspoken behavior at age twelve, Meg's mother had mailed a large box with photographs of Meg, Claire, and Jenny, and severed all blood ties. Following years of a sadistic exclusion by her mother, Meg clearly understood that whether or not she was the one in the wrong, it would be entirely up to her to mend fences.

Eventually, Meg made such attempts, letters, cards, phone calls, and flowers sent by FTD. But her mother had been so crushed that she would have none of it. And so she had died one day of an aneurysm, in her own stubborn way having the last laugh, leaving her daughter with a lingering, inescapable guilt she would carry for the rest of her life.

Talk about unfinished business. Meg empathized with Caleb Hill. The Ouija board had taken its place as a decorative item on Meg's piano. She noticed it each morning and again at night.

Jenny stopped by briefly on Saturday afternoon to wash her

uniforms and to tell Meg she'd spoken with her father, Jack.

"He's moving into a new house, Mom. And Claire and her boyfriend are helping him move."

"Did he grill you about your plans for college? What did he say about you living in a trailer?" Meg stood in the kitchen leaning against the counter, sewing the hems in the trouser legs of Jenny's uniform that she complained were just long enough to drag in the biscuit-maker's flour on the Burger Master floor.

"You know Dad. He thinks it's all your fault."

Meg gave a humorless snort. "Of course. Mom, the scapegoat. What did I do to ruin your life, ambition, and future plans this time?"

"He figured you started charging me rent to live here, which was why I moved out."

"Did you set him straight?"

"Hey! What are you doing with this Ouija board in the house? That's one of the few things you always told me not to do, play with the Ouija. Remember?"

"It was in the window of an antique shop. I thought I might put it in the log house."

"Good idea. Let the ghosts talk to each other. That old house gave me and Nell the creeps. I wish you wouldn't buy it."

"Why, Jenny? Even if I never renovated it, if I owned it then I'd never have to worry about someone putting a trailer park right outside my back door. If it's a cheap buy, I'd use it for a buffer zone, if nothing else."

They tossed ideas for Christmas gifts back and forth. What should Jenny buy for Jack, what could each of them give to Claire?

"And what do you want, Mom? Don't tell me nothing, like you usually do. I hate it when you say that, as if you're so unworthy you deserve nothing."

Meg pondered the twice-yearly question, Christmas and birthday. "A nice big fluffy washable pair of house slippers. My feet are always cold. Old age, no doubt."

"Speaking of which, you need to rinse your hair again. The silver's coming back in."

"What would I do without my Jenny? Thanks for telling me. But I thought I might let it go natural this time, like Aunt Chris."

"On Aunt Chris, it looks good."

"And on me, it doesn't?"

Jenny smiled mischievously, without needing to say another word.

"Incidentally, are you working tonight?"

"Four till closing."

Casually, Meg said, "Since you're working so late, do you want to stay here tonight?"

"No. I think I'll go home."

Home; so this was no longer the place her daughter thought of as Home. Jenny really wasn't a kid anymore. Not once had she asked Meg for money since she'd moved into the trailer. She and her friends were meeting their bills, electric heat and all.

Again, on a clear night a whistling wind whipped lacy sheets of snow around the house. The silvery light from a full moon cast eerie blue shadows on the ice-crusted blanket covering the lawn. Meg turned on the porch light and watched as veils of snow glinted past the light. Somehow the porch light made her home seem cozier, as if the lady of the house might be awaiting a guest.

Here it was, Saturday night. And she kept company with her dog and three cats, who were too intelligent to beg to go outside for their nightly foray. Really, if anyone were to ask, Meg Kites would have been the first to admit she needed some sort of social life.

But she was too old and too tired to play the field. Some of the divorced women she worked with met men at Happy Hours or cocktail lounges, a few had developed Internet romances. With Meg's luck, she'd meet another Warren.

But she had met Warren through a personal ad he had placed in the newspaper just before Christmas three years ago. The only ad she'd ever worked up her nerve to answer, and she'd hit the pot of gold, a man who died less than two years later.

She opened a diet cola, poured it in a glass, and went to see what was on television. No sooner had she found a movie than the lights flickered on and off several times, and then she was hit by a power outage.

After twenty minutes of sitting in the dark with her cats clustered around her, Meg realized the electricity was likely to be off for some time. She took two candles from the bookshelves and set one on either end of the coffee table. Lighting them, she waited until the cats settled down before reaching over to the piano for the Ouija board.

She hadn't done this since she was a kid at a slumber party in junior high. How did it work again? Did she ask the question first, and then put her fingertips on the edge of the planchette? Well, she doubted the fool thing would work, anyhow, so what difference did it make what technique she used?

Dr. Hollings' words came back to her: the Other Now, parallel dimensions, time-slips. Once she had read an explanation of Einstein's theory of relativity, about a man on a train who would eventually see himself passing on a parallel train, something to do with the speed of light. Much beyond her intellectual grasp, trying to understand the concept had given her a slight headache. She had felt like a mental dwarf, astonished that some brains worked with such theories as easily as she played a six-octave C-major scale on her piano.

Her lips curved in an involuntary grin. Look, Meg, she said to herself; if this is going to work, you have to get serious.

But she couldn't help but be amused by the setting: two lighted candles in a dark house, surrounded by three feline familiars, Ouija board and thee.

As she touched the planchette, nothing happened. She kept her fingers lightly balanced. "My name is Mary Margaret Kites. My friends call me Meg. Are you a friend?"

The planchette jerked forward slightly, startling her. Then it slid over to the corner inhabited by the word Yes, and came to a stop. Okay, that was spooky enough, for starters.

"I am interested in contacting Lucy Hill. Is she there?" As in, is anybody home? Really, Meg; get a life.

She closed her eyes and tried to mentally summon Lucy. Slowly, the planchette began to move, circling around and around very slowly as if gathering energy. "If you're a friend, who are you?"

It moved to the right, to the left, slightly right again, then in a swoop to the far right end, and back to the left a last time before it stopped: *F-a-i-t-h.*

"Faith? Are you Faith Hill, the woman who died in this house?" Again, the planchette went to the corner word Yes. "Did you solve the mystery, Faith? The mystery surrounding Lucy and Caleb?"

Patiently, Meg waited while the planchette spelled out *Not his.* What was she talking about, not his what? Not his mystery?

"Not his, Faith. What wasn't his?"

Child.

Meg felt chills tingle down her spine and raise the hairs on her arms and the back of her neck. "Whose child was Lucy carrying, Faith?"

Hurt.

The planchette seemed to go wild, moving across the board in such a frenzy Meg could hardly hold on to its edge.

Liar.

Grief.

And the instrument literally rushed off the end of the board and fell to the floor.

Meg sank against the back of the sofa, with the firm conviction she had toyed with depths of reality better left untouched. Hastily, she scooped up the board from the coffee table and the planchette from the carpet and tossed them into the back of her bedroom closet, slamming the door.

She washed her face and brushed her teeth by candlelight, let Cherry outside and waited by the door to let her back in before putting a disposable diaper on the dog. After washing the dog smell from her hands, she pulled on her flannel nightgown and went to bed, yanking the covers to her chin.

She stared at the dark ceiling, trying in vain to erase the cloying sense of uneasiness from her brief contact with the ghost who had identified herself as Faith Hill.

Chapter Eighteen

On a snowy Sunday morning, the church parking lot was almost empty, the small number of cars recently arrived for the eleven o'clock service dusted with fresh snow. Meg parked her car and moved gingerly over the rock-salted but icy path to enter the church.

She shook the hands of several deacons who waited to greet the incoming at the door, then walked down the aisle to take a seat in a pew near the front of the church.

As she might have predicted, the old people were here. The congregation's elderly must have felt so close to their day of reckoning that they were afraid not to come, to pray for a last helping of mercy, salvation hanging by a thread.

Well, Meg was in good company. Today she was more than a little concerned about the condition of her own soul.

She had a personal theory about damnation. It wasn't the huge, awful things most people would never think of doing or ever be accused of, such as murder, keeping one away from God's grace, but the jillion and one little things all mortals are prey to. What the Catholics called venial sins, as opposed to deadly or mortal sins. According to Father Cavanaugh's teaching in catechism class, venial sins were supposed to be easily forgiven, but Meg doubted it. With a proliferation of venial sins chipping away over a lifetime, how much forgiveness could be expected?

Sins like being responsible for a major fall-out with her own mother, a rift never to be reconciled. Or fiddling around with the Ouija board when she knew damned well she had no business flirting with such inventions condemned by the Church as doorways to the Occult.

A young, spritely woman led the audience in a series of hymns. Then a member of the congregation came to the stage and, while accompanying himself on guitar, sang a dreary song about Jesus dying on the cross, a song whose lyrics equated the Roman soldiers in charge of the crucifixion with Hitler's Gestapo.

At last, wearing one of his navy-blue suits, burgundy tie, and a benign expression, Pastor Smythe took the podium. "Good morning, Christians. Today's sermon will be the very essence of brevity, as I wrote it early this morning. But I'm pleased to see quite a few of my flock didn't choose to stay home in bed, on a day when it was tempting to do so. I know that it was all I could do, to appear before you this Sunday."

A polite titter from the congregation.

"My dear friends, the message today is on wizards that peep and mutter, a phrase taken from Scripture, Isaiah 8:19. And who are these wizards the Bible speaks of, who peep and mutter to us in our daily lives as we try to go about the business of doing the Lord's work? Well, friends, a multitude of wizards is all around us, more wily and beguiling even than the serpent in the Garden of Eden.

"Advertising pushes its products to make us slimmer, richer, sexier, happier, if only we'll buy. Politicians promise a miraculously transformed landscape in exchange for our vote. Riches, fame, popularity? You bet! All these things and more can be had, for a price."

A small chorus of Amens sounded throughout the sprinkling of old men in the audience.

"Yes, friends. For a price, because nothing comes free in this life. A small price of betrayal, a white lie, a malicious piece of gossip. What does someone else's reputation matter, as long as we've got ours? We're good people. Why, we're Christians! Doesn't that entitle us to special treatment in this hard old world of woe? Too many people today are espousing the Prosperity Gospel, that true believers can expect health and wealth, because we deserve it! We don't deserve a thing, if you ask me. Grace is a gift. God's love is a gift. Jesus is a gift. We've done nothing to earn it.

"Consider the plight of the madman, friends. How does he view reality? You've heard people say there's a mighty thin line between insanity and genius, haven't you? Those who rely on magic, chants, crystals, spirits from the other realm to tell them how to live. Channelers.

New Age. Wicca. Paganism. Foretelling the end of the world. Such arrogance!

"The Bible quotes Jesus as saying neither He nor the angels know when the end will come, but only the Father Himself. So I beseech you, brothers and sisters, follow the one King, renounce human greed and the acquisition of worldly possessions, take the right path, and love one another. And be whole, in this life and for all eternity.

"Let us pray. 'Dear Father, we have gathered in your house today to praise...'"

After the prayer, the collection was taken while the congregation sang *Jesus Is Tenderly Calling* as best they could, since the pianist had not shown up.

Pastor Smythe stood at the door to shake hands as today's remnant of his flock filed past. Meg thanked him for the sermon, went out to the car, shoveled the snow from the windshield with a whiskbroom, and drove away.

She stopped by the nursing home to inquire about Melody Hill Branscombe, only to be told Miss Melody had slipped into a coma the previous week and died in a Roanoke hospital. Meg left a large tin of English butterscotch toffees with specific instructions to the day nurse to give them to Nurse Williams, in memory of Miss Melody.

Driving home, she was amazed with herself when tears welled in her eyes, grief for the old woman she had met so briefly. Really, it wasn't simply a tired euphemism to say that Melody was in a better place. Any place would be an improvement compared to a life trapped in a wheelchair with no awareness of your surroundings. As long as there was a spark in the eye and an original thought in the brain, life had some value.

Selfishly, Meg thought of Melody's death and said to herself No help there; no more lucid moments to be had.

When she returned to her house, Meg pounded flour into a round steak with the edge of a heavy platter, to make Swiss steak with carrots, celery, tomatoes, onions and bouillon, to pop in the oven for an hour. It kept and reheated well, should Jenny decide to drop by in the next few days. She wouldn't be able to resist one of her favorites.

A vague suspicion had gnawed at Meg all during the church

service, something surfacing in her mind from the strange encounter with Faith Hill. Had it really been communication with a ghost rather than her own wacky imagination? She wished she could know for sure, so she wouldn't have the ancillary worry about Meg Kites losing her dwindling faculties. One glance at poor Melody had served to make the loss of mental control her worst fear.

Better to perish from lung cancer, she thought, lighting up.

Retrieving the box of stationery containing Faith's papers she had found in the attic, she carefully re-read each of the pages. This was the one that had tugged at her mind, the page dated April 15, 1905, the year Lucy either died or disappeared.

"What he has done, God forgive his soul, he did for me. But in my heart I will always know he loved her more."

He loved her more. Had Lucas Hill fallen in love with Lucy? Had he paid Lucy Hill to leave town, persuading her to abandon her five-year-old daughter and the husband she loved? But how could that have been possible, regardless of his powers of lawyerly persuasion?

Unless Lucas might have known something about Lucy's past, some malevolent bit of information she feared would destroy her if Caleb were ever to find out.

Meg gathered her thoughts before dialing Erin Sumptner's home in Richmond. "Erin? This is Meg Kites. I just found out today about Melody's passing. I called to offer you my condolences."

"Oh, my dear girl. How thoughtful."

"Will there be a funeral? I'd like to come."

"Oh, no. Who else would still be alive to attend? No, Meg. I requested she be cremated and her ashes scattered on her parents' graves. Faith and Lucas, that is. They were the only parents she'd known." Erin sighed and, when she tried to speak, her voice cracked. "I've not been well. Melody's death was a wrenching experience. Of course, as I'd known for the past several years, hers was no life at all. But now I am the last."

After an awkward moment of silence, Meg asked, "Did you receive the book with your mother's inscription?"

"I did. Thank you, Meg. I intended to send a note, but... It's funny, you know. Mother enjoyed reading romances by a Mrs. Southworth featuring spunky heroines who reminded her of Lucy. I placed the book you sent to me with those."

Meg considered the wisdom of revealing Faith's message from the Ouija board, but quickly released the thought. "I can't help but wonder why Lucy left, if she did. Or why Caleb allowed Melody to grow up believing Faith was her mother."

"It wasn't entirely Faith's doing. Caleb was away so much and, when he was home, he returned to the old house that he kept in Lucy's memory like a shrine. He couldn't bear the sight of Melody because she reminded him of Lucy."

"I found the letter Caleb sent to your mother, asking for any letters Lucy might have sent to her. Do you know whether she ever did?"

"Well, there are no letters here in Mother's papers, so if you didn't find them in Lucy's box of things, perhaps she did."

"Erin, I've been wondering about something else, since apparently your mother did know Faith fairly well. From what you've told me."

"Well enough for confidences to be given, I suppose. Faith believed Caleb's marriage to Lucy was ill-fated. She took it upon herself to contact Mother, to inquire whether there had been any hint of congenital defects or insanity in our family. If there had been, Caleb would have been within his rights to sever the engagement. In those days women were regarded as fragile, weak creatures, prone to nervous disorders like hysteria. They thought it was somehow connected to the womb."

"Did Lucas disapprove of the marriage as Faith seemed to, Erin, or do you know?"

"Well, I remember my mother saying she didn't like Lucas, not a bit. She described him as short, stocky, and belligerent, used to having his own way. He ruled Faith with an iron hand, and she was frightened of him. But those were Lucy's words. She didn't like Lucas, either, according to Mother."

"Did Lucas try to convince Caleb not to marry?"

"Mother said that, when she came to visit from Richmond and dined at Faith's home, Lucas seemed rather in awe of Lucy. She was the only one who would stand up to him. A regular firebrand. As I believe

I told you, when I was a child my favorite stories were the ones Mother shared about my Aunt Lucy. Though she had died, Mother made her seem very real to me. Her greatest compliment to me was when I did or said something reminding her of Lucy. They were very close, growing up."

Meg heard the change in Erin's voice, growing faint, nearly inaudible, and she realized it was time to end the conversation. "Erin, I'm sure the things in the house were for Melody to have. I don't know what I'll do with them, now."

"Sell them off to a dealer, if you wish. Oh! There was one thing I remembered after your visit with me. I recall Mother telling me how worried she had been about Lucy's mental state, when Ian was stillborn. It seems Lucy developed a sort of addiction to Lydia Pinkham's Vegetable Compound, which we know now was twenty per cent alcohol. You could buy most anything over the counter in those days, not so surprising when physicians were far and few between. Some women gave paregoric to their children, I understand."

"Well, I won't keep you. I'm so sorry about Melody. Please take care of yourself."

"Oh, I shall. And you'll be notified by my attorney prior to the auction of the Hill house."

Meg hung up, wondering if she'd just heard the wretched secret. Had Lucy become an alcoholic, turning to Lydia Pinkham's to assuage her grief from losing her infant son?

✱✱✱✱✱✱✱✱✱✱✱✱✱✱✱✱✱✱✱✱✱✱

Through a veil he had seen Honora, his new assistant, but he could not get through the barrier from the other side.

And the cabinet had been destroyed in the year 1916.

He had no choice but to search for another portal, an alternative path across the divide. As time passed, a strange sort of time without seconds or minutes or hours, he moved in a dark, solitary place, desperate to see a distant light in the emptiness, a brief flicker of hope that eventually he would find his way back.

But there was only silence, the terrible, suffocating, blind silence of an endless black void.

His own arrogance was his constant companion, a reminder of how he had thought to control the hidden forces of a world beyond the one to which he was born. Cruelly, he was made to understand how his pride and folly had been lethal, bringing destruction upon himself.

And upon the woman he would always love.

He sought to find her. He was consciousness without substance, will without power, his one hope to endure, to search for her. To survive.

Chapter Nineteen

"Good afternoon! Thank you for choosing Burger Master. How may we help you?" Meg smiled at the sound of Jenny's cheerful voice over the static of the drive-through speaker.

"It's only me. You want to get together with your old Mom, have dinner out, and hit the Mall for Christmas shopping?"

"When?"

"Saturday? I thought early-afternoon." At the tense silence from the other end, Meg deduced that Jenny was probably scheduled to work. "Oh, I'll have a large iced tea, unsweetened."

"One-twenty-nine. Please drive to the window." Jenny handed over the tall paper cup. "Gee, Mom. I'm sorry, but I have a date."

"A date? Who with, Jenny?"

"A friend of Joe's. His name is Owen, and he's a sophomore at the community college. I think I'm in love!"

"Where did you meet this guy?"

"At work! Which kills my theory that only nerds would work at Burger Master. He works at B.M. twenty hours a week, and he carries a full load at college."

"Where does Owen live, Jenny?"

"Pretty close to the trailer. He's sharing a garage apartment with another guy."

How convenient. "Have a good time, then. Maybe you can bring Owen by some time soon, so I can meet him."

"I will. I promise. I feel awful about not going shopping with you, though."

"Don't buy that emerald-green sweater for Claire, Jenny. I found one similar on sale."

The car behind her tooted its horn. With a jaunty wave, Meg drove away.

Well, now she had something more to add to her expanding catalogue of worries. Jenny thinks she's in love. Terrific.

Immediately, her mind began to spin possible outcomes – Jenny running away to elope instead of going to college – Jenny sobbing after Owen breaks her heart.

Her natural inclination to exhume bitter memories from her own past and pin them on her daughters gave Meg another reminder of her years of disappointment and grief where the men in her life were concerned. Really, she refused to dredge all of that up again. There was nothing to be gained and everything to lose, such as relative contentment and peace of mind.

She and Jack would never speak a civil word to one another again, and Warren was dead. So, what was the point? Both Claire and Jenny were entitled to make their own mistakes, without their mother's Cassandra-like predictions sucking the joy from their lives.

During the week she watched the Christmas sale inserts in the newspaper and wrote out a list of gift possibilities for Claire, Jenny, and her staff. There was no one else to buy for. She'd fallen into the habit of sending a zany card to Chris, one to her pastor, and another to Dr. Mitchum and wife, and that would be it. Oh, and one to Erin Sumptner.

On Saturday, shoppers jammed the Blue Ridge Mall, anxiously awaiting Santa's arrival from the North Pole. The mezzanine was filled with long lines of parents with their children in tow, determined to have a photo taken while, for the most part, toddlers and infants screamed in terror on Santa's lap. Meg felt the same way about Santa as she did about clowns: depressed.

Screeching carols blared from the loud speakers, people jostled one another in the stores. Meg didn't like to shop on the best of days, and after a few hours of fighting the crowds, she'd begun to feel claustrophobic and couldn't wait to get home.

When she paused to consider the last time she had been shopping with Jenny, months ago, she seemed to recall that they'd gotten short-tempered and had a rotten time. So it had really worked out for the best, Jenny preferring a date with Owen to accompanying her mother on another doomed shopping expedition.

Loaded down with scented candles, refrigerator magnets, and perfumed soaps for her staff, two sweaters and a book and a pair of gold earrings for Claire, seat covers for Jenny's Mazda to go along with a check for a few hundred dollars and a stretch pants and top ensemble to put under the tree...

She'd completely forgotten about the tree. She didn't know where she stored the ornaments after they'd moved into the house. Where was the tree stand?

Walking to her car parked on the outskirts of the huge lot, Meg couldn't think of anything much more pathetic than an image of herself sitting alone in her house, staring at a brightly-lit Christmas tree.

Who needed it? She dismissed the idea of having a tree this year. A wreath on the front door, a big red bow on the mailbox, the crèche on the window ledge, the Christmas angel on the coffee table. Bah, humbug.

After she had fed the pets, Meg laid out the gifts and an assortment of wrapping paper and ribbon in the living room. She tried to force herself into a holiday mood, but the task of wrapping the gifts made her feel lonely and wretched. She should have bought gift bags. Why hadn't she thought to orchestrate Christmas for her daughters in her new house?

One, because Jenny's schedule was insane and she couldn't plan from one day to the next. Two, because Claire would have had to drive seven hours each way and make room in her life for her mother's sentimental demands.

But there was a third, more personal reason. After years of planning and shopping and cooking and doing to make the holidays a memorable occasion, Meg was emotionally drained from the lifetime effort of inventing a festive spirit.

She carried the gifts to her bedroom to store in a garbage bag under the bed. Her arms were full and she couldn't catch the light switch. In the darkness of the room, her attention was drawn to the window. She stood absolutely still, closed her eyes for a moment, and looked again.

A soft amber light glowed in the upstairs window of the old house. She hadn't seen it there for some time. But tonight it had reappeared, as if someone inside waited for him to come home, directing his path.

She didn't know how she knew it, but she felt as certain that it was Lucy waiting for Caleb as she did of her own name.

She slid the last package into the garbage bag beneath the bed and went to stand at the window, hugging herself against the cool draft of air that had suddenly entered the room. Patiently, she gazed out at the light in the log house as if it were a lone, fragile beacon in the vast wilderness of an impenetrable night.

And then it came to her. Meg thought that somehow she finally understood: there was a missing, vital link they sought, something crucial they needed. Inexplicably, a sensation of deep recognition replaced her former feeling of resistance derived from a primitive fear.

With no thought of whether what she did was dangerous or irrational, Meg dug the Ouija board and its planchette from the back of her bedroom closet and took them into the living room. Again, she set the board on the coffee table and placed her fingertips on the edge of the planchette.

For several long moments, she sat in utter silence, her eyes closed and her conscious mind nearly free of thought. She neither formulated nor asked a specific question. Instead, she willed herself to sink into a meditative state of total receptiveness and calm.

The spirits can only get through to conduits open to them, Dr. Hollings had said. A psychic safety valve.

Soon the planchette glided in circles, as if in an effort to spell out letters. Meg refused to try and identify who it was seeking communication with her. Not this time...

When the planchette came to a brief pause, she opened her eyes and continued looking at the board almost without blinking.

F...i...n...d...h...e...r...g...r...a...v...e.

"Are you Caleb Hill?"

Yes.

"And you're looking for Lucy's grave?"

Yes.

"Where are you, Caleb?"

D...a...r...k.

"What is it, Caleb, that you and Lucy need?"

R...e...s...t...p...e...a...c...e.

"I'm going to try and talk with Lucy, Caleb, to ask where she is. I'll tell her you're trying to find her."

Meg followed the same procedure, sitting quietly with eyes shut, breathing slowly, suffusing her body with absolute calm. But the planchette would not respond.

"I'm calling for Lucy Hill."

Ten minutes passed, then twenty. But nothing surrounded Meg other than complete silence. Even her cats had moved to a different room of the house.

Meg got up, yawned and stretched, turned on a light. She opened her wallet and located the name and phone number of the medium recommended by Andrew Hollings.

She glanced at the clock. Nine-fifteen. It was worth a try.

Chapter Twenty

"Meg! How nice to see you in church two Sundays in a row." So said Pastor Smythe, as Meg shook his hand following the service and rushed out the door. Little did he know she'd come to Sunday worship service to say a prayer invoking spiritual protection for her soul.

Meg returned home to change clothes. At one o'clock, armed with explicit directions from Wilson County's main highway to the mountain community of Sweetgum Grove tucked back in a hollow, she set out to find the medium's house.

Midway on the two-lane highway she traveled each day from her house to the office, she turned left onto a graveled road. She made a right turn a mile and a half later, then an immediate left up Shagbark Mountain.

In the fall, with clusters of deep-red and yellow autumn leaves, the view would have been spectacular. Now she passed trees bowed with an accumulation of snow and ice. The tops of many had snapped off under the burgeoning weight, making the countryside look like a war zone, with giant jagged splinters outlined against a pewter-gray sky.

Well, at least the road up the mountain had been plowed, and Meg could see why as she passed an occasional house on either side, one with chickens scuttling about on a snow-crusted lawn. Whoever lived up here had to have access to the highway to drive to work.

When she spotted the aluminum mailbox with the name Sarah Grimes printed in black letters, she turned into the driveway and parked next to a Ford truck at the side of a double-wide mobile home whose deck was blanketed with droves of felines. Never before had Meg seen so many cats gathered in one place. They stared at her, collectively curious.

She got out of the car and walked to the steps, stopping to pet several cats. One white long-hair had sky-blue eyes, a beautiful animal Meg knew carried a recessive gene for deafness. Black cats, several ginger-striped Toms, black and whites, many gray tabbies, a few calicos genetically destined only to be female, all friendly and well cared for. Certainly not strays, with their plastic flea collars and gaze of secure contentment. A dozen plastic bowls of dry cat chow sat in a row.

The door opened before she knocked, and Meg peered through the storm door at a fortyish woman with bright blue eyes and a red kerchief over her brown hair, wearing a flannel shirt and a pair of bibbed overalls.

"Hi! Come on in."

She stepped into a warm living room featuring a woodstove in its center surrounded by overstuffed chairs, tables, and modern floor-lamps.

"Well, this is certainly cozy," Meg said, warming her hands by the stove. "My furnace went on the fritz not long ago, and I've been thinking about getting a woodstove for back-up."

"Not a bad idea. I save a bundle by burning wood. Have a seat. Would you care for a cup of tea? I just brewed a pot of Red Zinger."

"Yes, I would. Thank you."

While Sarah Grimes was in the kitchen, Meg had a few moments to survey the room. Lots of color photographs of cats sat on the television, shelves, and end tables. Books on tarot card reading, palmistry, auras, numerology made her wonder what she'd gotten herself into. Then she took a seat in the middle of the comfortable sofa.

Sarah placed a tray with teapot, two china cups, sugar and cream on the coffee table. She sat down in a rocking chair across from Meg and poured two cups of tea. "How do you take yours?"

"Straight."

"Also my preference. Well! You live alone, too, don't you?"

"How did you know that?"

"Takes one to know one. You also have cats."

"Three. And an old dog in Pampers who does nothing but urinate on the carpet, yelp all night, itch herself to death, and snorkel. Not a pleasant animal, these days. My youngest daughter's dog, so I've had to tolerate the inconvenience."

"That could be us, one day." Sarah Grimes chuckled, her calm blue gaze focused on Meg. "In answer to the question you were thinking but haven't asked, I'm forty-two, originally from Garden City, New Jersey, divorced from the lumberjack I moved down here for, one son who's in college in Florida. Anything else you'd like to know about me before we start?"

Meg tried to hide her discomfort, but without much success. "Do you make a living at this, Sarah?"

"The séances? Are you kidding?" Again, she laughed. "Lord, no! I'd starve to death. By trade I'm a photographer. Initially I was an art photographer, but nobody cared. So now it's animals, children, weddings, whatever pays. And I live frugally so I don't need much money to survive. After years of being caught in the middle of the advertising rat race, I like it this way."

"You're fortunate. I would bake cakes for a living, and tinker all day in my kitchen trying new recipes, if I could. I've always thought it might be fun to have a little catering business."

"Why don't you, then?"

"I'm tucking away Meg's Little Bake Shop as a retirement project. Guess I don't have quite enough courage to jump ship at my job just yet. However, the closer I get to age fifty-five, the more appealing it seems. As a matter of fact, I checked into it the other day and realized that with the three-hundred dollars I'd receive from my retirement pension at age fifty-five, I couldn't survive. Then there's medical insurance and life insurance benefits to consider, which I'd lose if I left my job and couldn't afford out-of-pocket."

Sarah smiled, sipping her tea. "Are you feeling less anxious about being here?"

"Yes, I am. I don't know what I expected, but you seem so down-to-earth and practical."

"I am that. But also psychic. Have been since I was a child. It's as much a part of me as hair color and height. Do you want to explain what brought you here?"

"As I told you over the phone, Dr. Andrew Hollings referred me," Meg began. Then she rambled on at some length about the old log house and its former occupants, the bits of Hill family history she'd pieced together, the communications from the Ouija board. She ended with her strong conviction that she was somehow expected to play an integral part in the final unfolding of the mystery of Caleb's disappearance and Lucy's eventual fate.

"I hear you saying you've come to believe there's a certain duty requested of you, one you must honor. And that would be?"

"He wants me to find her grave. He wants to rest in peace. Sarah, something's driving me to find out about this. I'm compelled to. Or maybe obsessed is a better word."

"You told me you've seen his ghost. And you think you may have seen her spirit as well?"

"Of course I can't be sure. But I think I did, one night. This phosphorescent, misty presence on the porch of the log house. An impression of a female presence, not as well-defined but quite different from his."

"Hmmm." Sarah seemed lost in thought for a few seconds. "She was Irish. And one of the manifestations is the sound of someone crying."

"Sobbing as if her heart will break. Wailing."

"In Gaelic, the word is *bansidhe*, which means fairy woman. We know it as banshee, a wailing woman who often portends death."

Meg rubbed her arms and said, "Whew! It feels downright spooky, when you put it that way."

Sarah grinned. "There are several reasons a spirit is kept earthbound. Hatred or revenge, a violent death that traps a spirit at the site of its demise. As for the ghost of the husband, he may crave justice to ease his deep remorse for something he believes he did or didn't do in this life. He wants something. He can't rest. As for your ghosts, there are many theories, but I'm sure Dr. Hollings mentioned as much to you. One is the psychic ether theory that says a haunting apparition emerges from mental activity, and survives in one or more dimensions between matter and mind."

Meg nodded, amazed when Sarah's words seemed to make perfect sense. "You know, I've wondered why nothing happened for the first four months my daughter and I lived in our new house. Dr. Hollings said the spirits might have been testing me."

"No doubt they were. You have to realize, Meg, that none of this might have been experienced by anyone else who had moved into your house. Just as poltergeists supposedly have a human catalyst, usually a child who lives in a house, so do spirits need a sensitive conduit from their dimension to the earthly plane. Interaction between a specific person and a certain place. You're a sensitive with definite psychic abilities." Sarah paused to finish her tea. Offhandedly, she said, "Though you've always denied it, haven't you?"

"Right again," Meg said ruefully, and found herself telling Sarah Grimes about her dream of her grandfather's death and her mother's subsequent terror, a memory she'd never before revealed to anyone.

"Something similar happened to me as a kid. I dreamed my best friend fell through thin ice when she was skating on a local pond and drowned. And she did. But my mother encouraged my psychic abilities. She was the same way, you see, and she seemed to know it was a gift we could only deny at our own peril."

"Well. Guess we need to figure our mother's attitude somewhere in the equation."

For a full minute, Sarah stared at her. But then her smile was gentle, her face soft.

Meg took refuge in the teapot and refilled each of their china cups. Instantly, she felt not only uncomfortable, but exposed. "You know what happened between Mother and... Don't you? I can tell."

"She loves you still, Meg. She always did. It's herself she's angry with. She asks me to beg your forgiveness."

Tears gushed from Meg's eyes. She didn't cry, she bawled like a baby. Sarah handed her a tissue, waiting quietly until she managed to release her grief and get her emotions under control. Finally, Meg managed to say, "I'm so sorry."

"Don't be. I'm glad I could help."

"You did. Very much."

In a business-like tone, Sarah said, "Let's get down to brass tacks. You wish to contact the spirit of Lucy Hill. You tried to contact her last night with the Ouija, but you weren't successful."

"Right." She slipped the antique ring from her finger and handed it to Sarah. "You asked for an object belonging to Lucy. This ring was hers."

"Good! Often this helps, having a personal object for its psychic vibrations. It's called psychometry. I'll need your cooperation. All you have to do is not speak unless I ask a direct question."

"You don't use a crystal ball, or candles or anything?"

"I don't need a bunch of bunk. Now we begin."

Fascinated, Meg watched as the woman seemed to relax every muscle in her body, emanating a sense of tranquility. A serene expression settled on her face. It was like self-hypnosis, Meg thought, a self-induced trance state. Lucy's ring was enclosed in Sarah's right hand.

When she spoke, her voice sounded different, low and deep, almost guttural. "I call upon my spirit guide, Jabal Sunaghanji, to lead me into the other realm. Jabal, I am seeking Lucinda Kelly Hill. We believe she may have departed from the plane in the year 1905. We are calling for a woman named Lucy Hill."

Sarah began to breathe heavily. Her body became stiff and rigid, her face contorting into an agonized expression. "She weeps! She weeps because she died and left her small child motherless. Lucy, Lucy Hill. We are here to help you. Your husband Caleb searches for your grave. Lucy, where do you abide in the Hereafter?"

Sarah's hands rested on the table, but suddenly her right hand flew open and Lucy's ring popped out of her palm and landed in the tea tray.

Startled, Meg's eyes had riveted on the ring and, when she glanced at Sarah again, the woman was coming out of her trance. She yawned and stretched her arms languidly, as if waking from a long, relaxing sleep.

"Are you okay?" Too late, Meg realized she had forgotten the medium's request for silence.

"I saw her, Meg. She was buried in a white, blood-stained nightgown. Red hair. She said you should look for the cairn. But I sensed no urgency. Evidently, it's not time yet. I can't say why. She said to look for the cairn. Her only words."

"Cairn?"

"Also originally from Gaelic, when it was spelled, c-a-r-n. A cairn is a pile of rocks."

"She's buried under a pile of rocks? But that could be anywhere!"

"I'm sorry, but that's all I heard." Sarah covered her mouth, stifling a yawn.

"Well, what do I do now?"

"Wait. You'll find it, I'm sure. She will lead you there in her own time."

"You didn't hear anything else?"

"Not hear, exactly. Saw is more like it. Three words written on darkness like chalk on black velvet. Caleb magic cabinet."

Meg almost jumped from the sofa. "Caleb was a magician! He and Lucy took his traveling magic show on the road!"

"When did you say he disappeared?"

"It was in 1916, according to his sister-in-law's papers found in the attic of my house. He was gone for eight months and they couldn't find him, and then his brother Lucas had a memorial service for him, and my vet said he remembers attending the funeral with his mother as a little boy, and they buried an empty coffin." Meg stopped and, replaying what she had just said, began to laugh. "Dear Lord, do I need a life, or what? These people have begun to seem more real to me than the people I see every day at my office. Not a healthy sign, no doubt."

"Don't be frightened by it. The day will come when you will remember them as you now remember old friends. When your part in the Hill family mystery is finished."

As Sarah yawned again, Meg rose from the sofa and took a step toward the door. "Sarah, I'd like to pay you for the séance."

Stretching, Sarah got up from her rocking chair. "Twenty dollars. I'm out of cat food."

"How many cats do you have?"

"Who can remember? It varies from day to day. I have a core group of seventeen. The rest drift in and out of my life. The kids in the neighborhood call me the Cat Lady, and they bring strays. I let them all in at night when it's cold. They heap themselves on my bed. We have a great sleep."

Taking leave, Meg extended her hand. "Thank you again."

Sarah waved from the doorway. "I accept referrals. Send your friends!"

Driving back down Shagbark Mountain, Meg pondered the message supposedly from Lucy Hill. Then she had died and, according to what Sarah Grimes had said about a spirit being trapped in an earthbound place, she may well have died violently.

Had Lucy committed suicide, then? And if so, how had she ended her life?

One thing that greatly impressed Meg had been Sarah's casual attitude about the spirit world. Obviously, she was not embarrassed about having a spirit guide or conducting a séance for a perfect stranger on a Sunday afternoon, contacting a spirit she had known nothing about other than the fact that Lucy Hill had been Irish and had a husband named Caleb.

There was no way Sarah could have known that Caleb was involved in magic, not unless what she had told Meg was the absolute, unvarnished truth, and those three words had appeared in her mind during the séance: Caleb magic cabinet.

Sarah Grimes was a true clairvoyant, one who could see or intuit people and events far beyond the normal range of perception. Somehow Meg was convinced that the twenty dollars she had given to Sarah might well prove to have been one of her wisest investments.

Whatever her other achievements in this life, the woman certainly had the unique power to weave an extraordinary spell. Dr. Hollings had recommended Sarah as an exceptional medium, and now Meg could see why.

Odd, how the crushing feeling of grief at the pit of her stomach whenever she thought of her mother had gone away. It had been replaced by a sense of belonging, a feeling of warmth and peace.

Yes, Sarah Grimes had accomplished so much for Meg.

The car began to slip on the pavement, the falling snow mixing with sleet. She was thankful that, in a few more miles, she would be home.

Even at high speed, the windshield wipers fought a losing battle, with ice accumulating on the glass around the two swipes the wipers were barely keeping clear.

Would the snow never stop? Meg wondered how she was supposed to look for anything, much less a pile of rocks, buried under eight inches of hard-packed snow.

Chapter Twenty-One

As if her life had not already taken another peculiar turn, Meg was astonished when events became even more surreal.

The Department of Social Services Christmas party, scheduled for the afternoon of December twentieth, was an obligation she'd been dreading for weeks. With corny quips, the staff members exchanged gag gifts. The worst was a Hawaiian bra made of coconut shells for a flat-chested Eligibility Technician. The gift to Meg from her staff was a toy telephone that said, "Sorry. Nobody home."

Eggnog flowed freely. Some of the young male staff members seemed so happy and upbeat that Meg began to wonder whether the eggnog was spiked. Christmas carols played from Dina Richards' boom box, currently a jazz medley performed by Kenny G.

Fran Giddings had brought in her annual holiday offering, elaborate trays of assorted homemade cookies. Others had contributed chips and dip, salted nuts, tea sandwiches, a vegetable platter with a choice of ranch, French onion, or blue cheese dressing. A ginger ale and raspberry ice cream punch floated maraschino cherries in a large crystal bowl, a frothy concoction that was so sweet you couldn't drink it, like drinking liquefied cotton candy.

For the past hour, the staff had managed to force a small measure of gaiety and laughter in a semblance of holiday camaraderie. But when an uninvited guest, a dour-faced ghost from the past, timidly skulked through the door, a hushed silence fell over the room like a funereal shroud.

Meg couldn't believe her eyes when they lighted upon none other than Norman Feder. Chastened, he asked to speak to her privately. Suppressing a sigh, she donned a smile and led him to her office. As soon as she closed her door, he sat down, wearing an expectant expression that she knew could only spell trouble in spades for Meg Kites.

"Mr. Feder, I'm so sorry things worked out for you the way they did," she began,

"I'm here because I want my old job back. Please!"

She had to glance away from the crazed look in his beady brown eyes. Never once, not once in all the years she had known him, had it occurred to her that Norman Feder might have a dangerous side. Annoying, passive-aggressive, vengeful, infuriating, yes – all of the above. But never dangerous.

Suddenly she wished she hadn't been so compliant about honoring his request for privacy. If only she'd ushered him over to a corner of the lobby, where other people were within earshot. Her mouth was dry. She said nothing.

"Meg, you know I've rendered faithful service to this department. You can vouch for my integrity with the County Manager. There must be something you could do to help me."

"Marty's the Rock of Gibraltar where you're concerned, Mr. Feder. Have you tried to appeal to him directly?" She picked up the phone, thinking this might be a way to get off the hook. "I could call him for you. Maybe if you spoke with him..."

"No! He refuses to accept my calls. Meg, I'm desperate. There's no reason to get out of bed in the morning. You don't understand my predicament. Social work was my life! Without it, I might as well be dead!"

To emphasize his words, he pulled a revolver from the pocket of his jacket and held the barrel to his temple, his finger poised on the trigger, his eyes trained on Meg.

Her heart pounding, Meg summoned the skills from her years of empathy training and counseling. "Norm, that's no solution, and you know it. Put down the gun and we'll talk this through."

He looked at her skeptically, but then he did as she asked, placing the weapon on her desk but easily within his reach.

"That's better," Meg said, her eyes on the gun. "You're much too intelligent to...well, please talk to me. I'm listening."

Norman Feder's lizard-like tongue darted from his mouth, licked his thin lips. "You can't understand what I've been going through, job interview after job interview. I even tried to become an exterminator. They wouldn't hire me even for that. I've sunk so low they refused to allow me to rid the world of vermin!"

"You're saying that you haven't had much luck with interviewing. But Norm, you have to keep trying and surely..."

"The only job I was considered for was night desk clerk in a shabby motel. Little better than a rooming house, for derelicts and bums in Roanoke. A flop-house for street people!"

"And you turned it down?" Meg was incredulous, despite her awareness that she needed to remain impassive in the face of the man's agitation. "Norm, you could clerk and earn money until a job suitable to your education and experience comes along."

"It's not the money. I don't need the money. I need to feel useful and productive. Meg, I loved my investigator job, I did. And then Marty fired me!"

As Meg tried to think of what to say next, she watched in disbelief as he jumped from the folding chair beside her desk, picked up the gun, aimed it at his head and pulled the trigger.

Click!

There he stood in her office, Norman Feder. With a greasy, devious smile spreading across his wizened, ferrety face.

"Get out," she said as she stood up. "How dare you come here and play my sympathies. If you want to pretend to be suicidal, do it on your own time." She pushed past him, opened the door, and stalked out to the lobby.

"Time!" he shrieked, trailing her down the hall. "Time is all I have. Thanks to you. It's your fault I lost my job, I know it is. You never liked me!"

Again, his presence caused an uncomfortable lull amidst the merry-makers. Horrified, they stared at Norman Feder as, once again, he pointed the gun to his temple and pulled the trigger once, twice...

...and blew his brains all over the white walls of the County Department of Social Services before crumpling to the lobby's newly installed teal-blue indoor-outdoor carpet.

Following a stunned silence, pandemonium broke loose, with women crying hysterically in intimate groups, holding one another. Someone thought to turn off the boom box in the middle of Alvin and the Chipmunks chirping Jingle Bell Rock.

Meg stared at the top half of Mr. Feder's skull that had landed under the Christmas tree, and insanely wondered whether she should check his pulse for signs of life.

One of the staff hurried to alert the Sheriff's Office. Meg placed a call to Marty, saying she needed his permission to close the office early because Mr. Feder had blown his head off at the staff Christmas party and people were upset.

"Shit! Well, isn't this going to look hunky-dory in the newspapers?"

"Who cares, Marty? You weren't here. You didn't see how his eyes glittered with insanity. And what do you know? I'm closing the office until the twenty-eighth. That's seven days. You can always fire me if you want, but you'll have to run it past the local welfare board. Oh, and I want new carpet installed in the lobby and the walls repainted before any of my staff sets foot in here again. Have a nice Christmas, Marty." She slammed the phone down in his ear.

Sirens rent the air outside the building. A team from the rescue squad wheeled in a gurney, wrapped the body in a blue-plastic bag and rolled it out the door. Sheriff's deputies arrived to interview the staff. They needed statements.

Meg reached down to unplug the tree lights. "Fran, ask the staff to come out here. I have an announcement."

Joanne went to the intercom. "All staff, please report to the lobby. All staff."

After they were assembled, many of the women still in tears, Meg said, "I'm sure no one needs to say that this was one of the most unpredictable and horrifying events to ever happen in our lives. I have no words of wisdom to impart. Who would? The only thing I could do was seek Marty's permission to close down the department until December twenty-eighth. Please go home, try to enjoy Christmas with your families and loved ones, and say a prayer for Norman Feder. We can lock up and leave now.”

Fran Giddings was on her way out, loaded down with dress boxes filled with extra cookies, when she stopped by Meg’s office. “What should we do about the tree?”

“I’ll take off the ornaments before I go, and call maintenance to haul it off while we’re gone.”

“What about the clients, Meg?”

“They don’t receive their food stamps until the twenty-ninth. If anything else comes up, they’ll just have to deal with it until we’re back. Don’t worry about the clients, Fran.”

Gradually, when law enforcement had obtained the needed information, the office began to empty until Meg was the only one left. She removed the ornaments, placing them in several cardboard boxes to be wrapped and stored away later. Then she unstrung the lights.

It was seven-thirty before she stepped in the door of her house. The cats milled around her, yowling for their dinner. As she emptied dry chow into the plastic bowls, tears streamed from her eyes.

As long as she lived, she knew she could never expunge the gruesome scene of Mr. Feder’s suicide from her memory. To have wanted to embrace death, he must have felt he was beyond any possibility of hope, and his life had become utterly pointless.

Which threw yet another light on Lucy’s decision to end her own life, if indeed that was what had happened.

Chapter Twenty-Two

With an unexpected week's hiatus, Meg tried to keep busy in a fruitless attempt to scour the hideous scene of Norman Feder's death from her mind. She couldn't escape self-blame, holding herself responsible at least in some small measure for pushing him from his comfortable two-windowed office, for tossing him into the streets as welfare fraud investigator.

But Marty was also at fault. He could have put Mr. Feder in charge of the Xerox room at the Courthouse, scheduling maintenance of the machines and contacting all departments to inquire about the need for paper supplies, something, anything rather than firing him. Marty was an excellent manager, but not known for his compassion. Maybe that was why he was an excellent manager.

Two days before Christmas, she called Claire long-distance in Maryland, and then Jenny at the trailer, conveying her love and holiday greetings. To occupy herself, she drove to the library for several novels and a new book on Scandinavian sweater patterns, cleaned the kitchen and bathroom from stem to stern, gave Cherry Lamb a bath in the tub, and rinsed her own hair dark-brown.

She went to church for Sunday services, praying for Norman Feder's soul during silent prayer. In penance, she attended the special cantata at the church on Christmas Eve and forced herself to stay afterward to participate in the gift exchange. She brought a tape of carols by country artists to a man she didn't know and received a set of flimsy kitchen dishtowels from a woman whose name she couldn't remember.

If she'd been more active in the church, going on their hayrides in the autumn, attending various potlucks and holiday celebrations, she realized she'd have known her fellow church members. But such socializing was not for Meg. At the first opportunity, before refreshments were served, she darted out the door of the fellowship hall to her car.

Celebrating Christmas alone with the dog and cats was another dismal affair. After opening the few gifts from her daughters, in a continued effort to put her enforced vacation time to good use, Meg took the key to the log house from its hook in the kitchen. She pulled on boots and a jacket and tromped over the snowdrifts to unlock the door, flashlight in hand.

She wanted to examine the old woodstove and see if it might be in good condition, to use as a hedge against next winter's power outages. Jenny had promised to stop by for fruitcake and eggnog with her new boyfriend in the afternoon. Maybe she could persuade them to help her lift the woodstove from the log house to her own basement.

She unlocked the door and stepped into the living room, immediately turning on the flashlight. Get the job done and get out of here, she told herself.

First, she studied the stovepipe, only to learn that it was securely cemented into the chimney. It would have to be moved professionally by someone who knew woodstoves. And how heavy was this old stove?

Training the beam of the flashlight onto the stove itself, she could find no visible cracks or signs of damage. Even with age, ordinarily a cast-iron stove doesn't wear out, or so she'd heard.

Several questions begged answers, such as the safety of venting the stove into the existing flue in her basement, into which the oil furnace was already vented. But she wouldn't use the stove if the furnace was operating, only when the electricity was off.

She opened the door on the front of the stove and shone the light inside. Reaching in, she took out some papers only slightly charred along one edge, thinking the former occupants must have used the stove for burning trash as well as heat. The missing pages from Lucy's journal! How long had they been in the stove, and who had thrown them here in an apparent effort to burn her words away, to destroy them forever?

Brushing soot away from the dozen or so pages, Meg hurried from the house, locking the door behind her and, using her own footprints, walked quickly across the back yard to the kitchen. She pulled off her jacket and boots, cramming her feet into the fluffy slippers from Jenny, sat down at the table and, her excitement mounting, began to read. Although the entries were not dated, Meg suspected that these pages contained a record of the last days of Lucy Hill's life.

"I have failed Caleb by not giving him a healthy son. My greatest desire is to bear him another child. I have visited with Miss Esther, the midwife, who has told me to spend time each day near the springs, to increase the chance our next child will also be a son. She has given me a potion to take in the mornings. Jayne's Carminative seems to cure my morbid mental state."

Meg remembered what Erin Sumptner's mother had told her, that when Lucy's second child was stillborn, she resorted to strange medicines and practices.

Impulsively, she picked up the phone and dialed the home of Dr. Mitchum, who was celebrating Christmas with his daughter and her family visiting from Charlottesville.

"Dr. Mitchum, I had an ulterior motive for calling, not just to wish you a Merry Christmas," she said. "But have you ever heard of something called Jayne's Carminative?"

"My word! I haven't heard it mentioned in years. Jayne's was touted as a miracle cure-all fifty years ago or more."

"Well, what was in it, do you know?"

The elderly veterinarian snorted derisively. "Alcohol and opium, that's what it was. Made addicts out of poor, unsuspecting people with no access to modern-day medical care. Wouldn't feed such a potion to animals, much less to humans. But people swore by it then."

Dear Lord! Opium! "Well, thanks, Dr. Mitchum. I'll be in to see you in a few weeks to have my daughter's new baby-boy cat neutered, much as I hate to do it."

"You brought home another stray, did you." A statement, not a question, followed by a low chuckle.

"Not this time. Jenny's boyfriend gave her a kitty for Christmas."

"I'd say to Mother, best to watch that budding relationship. From one animal lover to another, you know."

Ringing off with a Happy New Year to Dr. Mitchum and family,

Meg poured a cup of orange juice and returned to Lucy's words.

"The doctor says I suffer from neurasthenia. I am fearful each day, nervous. I feel hot and then so cold I shiver. My heart beats too fast by twice. It has been a year now since Ian died, and Faith chides me, saying it is impolite to grieve so long. Caleb is not with the railroad now, as his show enjoys a resounding success. He has employed a new assistant to take my place until I am feeling myself again. I wish he were here. I miss him so."

"A terrible thing has happened, so terrible I cannot write of it. I fear I may be with child. If only I could travel to Richmond and confer with Catherine, I know something could be done for me in the city."

"I must arrange not to bear this infant."

Lucy's neat handwriting had turned into a haphazard scrawl across the pages. Some of her words were difficult to read, and Meg could only decipher them in context.

"Suddenly I have grown afraid of Miss Esther. I have come to believe she has cast an evil spell upon me."

"Only this evening I felt a strong urge to push Melody's fair head beneath the bathwater. For some time I have felt myself growing apart from my daughter. She is happier with Faith than she is with me."

On the next page Lucy had crossed out several sentences with black ink, obliterating the words. But then, on the following page, came another entry.

"At long last, Lucas had agreed to help me on condition that Caleb never learn of it. He is giving me quinine, a few small doses each day. He promises it will work, but may require some weeks."

"Melody is always with Faith now. Lucas moved her playthings into town to their house, until this dreadful ordeal has ended. I have no strength. The grounds are untended, the house neglected. I take no food."

"I ingest more quinine than is prudent, I know. But this must be done quickly. I cannot endure more."

"Caleb has written that he will be home in two weeks. I know now that I can neither live with nor without this child who grows in my womb. When Caleb is here, I must behave as if filled with joy."

"I am ill, too weary to write these words."

And the last entry: "God help me, but I wish his brother were dead!"

An icy recognition slowly seeped into Meg. Finally, she'd stumbled across a missing clue, and the truth had dawned on her as surely as the rising sun points fingers of light above the eastern horizon.

Not Caleb's child, but Lucas's child! Why else would Lucas Hill have given his sister-in-law quinine? Meg had read somewhere that women once used quinine to bring about a spontaneous abortion, but she had always believed it was an old wives' tale.

And poor Faith had written that, in her heart, she would always know he loved her more, and what Lucas had done, he had done for Faith. Had the quinine killed Lucy, or affected her mind to such an extent that she forced her own hand to turn against herself, and perhaps against her unborn child, the infant she refused to bear?

Ironically, the answer to the mystery Meg had sought now made her wish she had never found it. Imagining Lucy's terror, Meg felt the sting of unbidden tears.

And then, when she thought of Norman Feder, she began to cry. When was Jenny going to get here, damn it? Meg no longer wanted to be alone.

Chapter Twenty-Three

In the mailbox on Tuesday, Meg received a brief letter from Chris Phlegar in Richmond. Chris and her daughter Allison were preparing to visit the grandparents in Pensacola on the annual pilgrimage for quarts of preserved figs. She promised to call Meg to wish her a happy new year upon their return.

Enclosed with the letter but without comment was an obituary from the Richmond newspaper. Erin Sumptner had died, four days ago. Meg read the obituary twice. Indeed, a distant nephew who now lived in Arkansas was listed as surviving kin, the probable heir to the Hill acreage. Somehow the news of Erin's death did not fill her with the same remorse she'd experienced after Melody Hill Branscombe's passing. At least Erin had enjoyed a rich, full life. No children, true, but two husbands who'd preceded her in death.

Meg would return to work the next day, and she felt that tomorrow couldn't arrive too soon. Anything to get her mind off her prolonged obsessive-compulsive preoccupation with the Hill family.

It didn't help a whit that Owen, Jenny's new beau, had not impressed Meg in the slightest. Another version of Brianna's Joe – shiftless, sullen, and bordering on rudeness. He'd scarcely spoken two words directly to Meg in the brief time he had allowed Jenny to visit with her own mother on Christmas Day. All the more inexcusable, since they were driving to Roanoke to see Owen's parents after they left Meg's house. It was a safe bet that Owen hadn't slouched around like a bored zombie with his family.

Meg found an outfit to wear to the office, took a bath and washed her hair. She went to bed early, anxious for the time spent at home with only her own churning thoughts for entertainment to come to a halt.

Her resolutions for the New Year were to launch a fitness program, lose the rest of the weight, quit smoking, and meet some new and interesting people she might one day call friends.

Again, as she fell off to sleep, pointlessly she wished that Chris Phlegar didn't live so far away.

The cats woke her at six a.m. Stumbling from bed to the bathroom, she looked at her own blurred reflection as she started to splash cold water on her face. In the thin patina of dust, toothpaste droplets, and smudges on the bathroom mirror, a message had been written by a ghostly hand: Find her.

As if nothing out of the ordinary had occurred, Meg washed the mirror with Windex and paper towels. Then she performed her usual morning tasks, getting dressed, applying make-up and fixing her hair, packing a few low-fat items from the refrigerator for lunch.

Before she left the house, she went through the service listings of the telephone directory and called a heating company in the area featuring a crude drawing of a woodstove in the Yellow Pages ad.

"What's the latest possible time you could come to move the stove?"

"Close up at five."

"But I don't get off until five, and can't be home much before five-thirty. Can you send a man out on Saturday?"

"Not open Saturday."

"Then I'll unlock the log house when I get home tonight, and I'll leave my basement door open. Could you do it tomorrow?"

"Yes, Ma'am."

"Thank you," Meg said, a slight testiness to her tone. "Just leave the bill in my mailbox."

"One thing, though. You ought to lay in a supply of green wood this spring and let it season before autumn. Not a good idea to burn green wood in those old stoves."

"Thanks for the tip."

Going out to her car, Meg wondered what it was about these people in Wilson County – nope, yep, maybe, probably not. It wasn't too late to put her house on the market and move into town, closer to her office.

But ghosts or not, she liked her little house. She guessed she'd gotten up on the wrong side of the bed, as her mother used to say, and today she was just mad at the world.

Not that Caleb's message had done much to improve her mood. One thing she was going to do: throw out that damnable Ouija board.

Father Cavanaugh's warning from so long ago had been accurate, after all. She should never have started with this nonsense.

Chapter Twenty-Four

Meg arrived for work fifteen minutes late, thanks to crawling thirty miles an hour behind a slow-moving log truck whose high load blocked a view of oncoming traffic and prevented her from passing it for a twelve-mile stretch.

An unnatural silence suffused the offices of the County Social Services Department, not that it would last for very long. With the doors shut abnormally long, the lobby was quickly filling up with decrepit elderly, single moms and their screaming infants, families with small children.

Several young couples with hostile, furtive expressions looked perfectly fit, capable of reporting for duty at some type of gainful employment. Was the handout of a monthly pittance worth the humiliation? How would they react to sanctions imposed by Workfare?

There seemed to be more and more out of work as the months rolled by. The unemployed, the underemployed, the working poor, those on disability – human service agencies had many compassionate terms for the down and out.

But Meg suspected she and her staff dealt mostly with the lazy, unmotivated, and unambitious. Malingerers; shades of Norman Feder and those he chalked off as nothing but wastrels.

Maybe Mr. Feder had been accurate. Maybe their clients were wastrels, and Meg, Fran, and the others with half a heart had squandered their lives on tea and sympathy.

Some of the young men she spotted in the lobby wore baseball caps. She'd have bet they drove pick-up trucks and ran the roads all day, when they weren't here to get their food stamps and other freebies they seemed to regard as their rightful due. After all, wasn't America the land of the free, where people looked after their own?

One of the vehicles parked in a client slot had sported a bumper sticker reading Send 'em back to where they come from! Buy American! Meg took this as an illiterate allusion to Latinos, Asians, African-Americans, et cetera. Apparently, one of their clients took personal offense at the immigration problem.

Why did they care? Meg wondered. Having defiantly refused to work for a living, their tax dollars weren't even addressing the issue.

The old saw about Charity beginning at home came to mind. She felt infuriated by her own sour attitude, and realized she didn't want to be here. Anywhere but here.

"Good morning, Joanne," she said, stopping by the receptionist's window. "How was your Christmas?"

"Better than the staff party," Joanne replied. "The mood around here isn't up to snuff today, Meg. Just thought I'd warn you. Be prepared."

"Thanks. Put a call through to the County Manager for me, would you? I'll be in my office."

She intended to give him hell for foisting Mr. Feder off on her. Marty had avoided the man, placing Meg in the unenviable position of patching things up and, while not re-hiring him, trying to make him feel benignly grateful about having been royally screwed. And now she'd been stuck with the lingering guilt, not Marty, when he was the one who was paid big bucks to deal with this sort of personnel dilemma.

Though she noticed that the carpet had been replaced and the white walls repainted. First, she would thank him for his prompt response to her inflamed demands.

The staff glided in and out of her office all morning. Most had questions they could have handled easily on a good day, none actually requiring Meg's advice, decision, or recommendation. People were feeling frail and incompetent today. Small wonder; so was she.

Fran Giddings had brought in a platter of Million Dollar Fudge opulent with pecans and marshmallows, parked next to the coffee machine. Shelving her diet resolutions, Meg ate three pieces with four cups of coffee, thinking she'd leave today's brown-bag lunch in the staff refrigerator for tomorrow.

Good old Fran, the nurturer. Meanly, Meg thought again that such kindness and heart were wasted on wastrels in this line of work.

Perhaps the federal welfare legislation intended to reform the system would call for new staff people trained in the manner of Marine Corps drill instructors. Make it so unpleasant to ask for food stamps that a person with a shred of personal dignity would do anything for an honest buck, even toil at Burger Master.

During the brief Christmas Day visit, Meg noticed when Jenny didn't once mention working her way up to management or applying for a company scholarship to college. Not a good sign, if her daughter's former enthusiasms could be so easily damaged by the appearance of an Owen in her life.

Steve Tomazcyk knocked on the door frame. "Meg? See you a sec?"

"What's the problem, Steve?" Thankfully, she gave him her full attention, the cute blond kid fresh out of college, former Eagle Scout. Steve's younger sister was a child with Down's Syndrome, her photograph proudly displayed on his desk. Just a sweet, kind-hearted boy who wanted to accomplish good in this world...

"Seems this family got a three-thousand-dollar insurance reimbursement they conveniently forgot to declare."

"Fire? Were they burned out of their trailer, or what?"

Steve offered an ironic grin. "Though I can't prove it, seems I remember her bitching about their Pontiac Cutlass not working in reverse gear. Rumor has it from another client in the trailer park that he ran the car off a cliff in a drunken snit, to collect the insurance money."

"We don't have the resources to get into that one, Steve. Just deem them ineligible on the grounds of an evaluation of their undeclared assets. God, what some people don't think of."

"Now they're driving a new Ford Ranger. Wonder how they got that?"

"Beats me. Won the lottery? Include the Ford Ranger in the assets statement."

"And here I am, trucking around in a six-year-old vehicle."

"Mine's ten years old. The longer you remain in this job, the lower down the rungs of success you go. Bear that in mind.”

With a chuckle, Steve left to complete the requisite reams of paperwork, so irksome that it would have been tempting to most workers to take the easy way out and keep their mouths shut.

“Mrs. Kites, the County Manager, line three.”

She grabbed the phone before she gave herself a chance to rehearse the intended tirade. “Marty, thanks for fixing up the office for us.”

Obviously cowed, Marty said, “Jeez, Meg. That was the least I could do. I can’t express my apologies strongly enough. This business was my fault. You know it, and I know it. If I’d met with the man, maybe he wouldn’t have appeared at your door. I’m really sorry.”

“Well, heck-fire. You took the wind out of my sails. I was going to read you the riot act.”

“No need. Mea culpa. Incidentally, the Supervisors approved December thirtieth and January second as County holidays. So you and your staff will have a four-day break.”

“Thanks.” She guessed. Four more days at home, to go a little bit crazier.

Claire telephoned on New Year’s Day, interrupting Meg from the football game on television in which she had no interest and had turned on only for the human sounds of cheering.

“Happy New Year, kiddo! What did you do to celebrate last night?”

“Ugh. Drank too much wine, partied too long. John and I went to my boss’s house. Most of the staff showed up. Anything but fun.”

“How is John?” What she really wanted to ask was, have you set a date to be married yet? After all, they’d been together three years.

“He’s fine. We’re doing okay. Last weekend we helped Dad move into his new house.”

“Is it nice?”

“Bigger than your house, from the photos you sent. Too big for one person. He has a lot of stuff I recognized from our old house. Didn’t you get anything in the settlement, Mom?”

"Hell, no. I had to walk away nude. But I don't care. He can have it all. I hope it makes him happy."

"Even so, it made me angry. It's not fair."

"The only thing that really pissed me off, as you know, was when he absconded with the photo albums, all the pictures of you kids growing up. If I'd taken them, I'd have had duplicates made, for him."

"I'll try to do that for you, if I can ever get them out of his hands for a few weeks."

"How was Christmas? Did you do anything special?"

"Had Christmas dinner at my apartment for Dad. Listen, I need to clear the air about something. Thanks for the nice sweater and earrings. But what was the book supposed to mean, about having a child after thirty? You seem to keep forgetting I'm only twenty-eight, Mom, not quite twenty-nine."

"Well, I'm sorry, darling! Of course. Ten years between you and Jenny. I'm not trying to make you lose a year, believe me. Maybe I was counting the year I was pregnant with you, I don't know."

"But about the book. Was it a hint? If so, you certainly weren't very subtle."

"I thought you'd appreciate it, Claire. The author discussed the very issues I thought you must be struggling with."

"Who's struggling, you or me?"

"What is that supposed to mean?" Meg felt her blood pressure rising, and she couldn't let it happen because of a disagreement with Claire, her first child, the baby she almost never had a chance to spend time with, now all grown up and...

"A woman's femininity isn't defined by whether or not she procreates, you know."

"Well, excuse me for wanting grandchildren!"

"Who's to say I'd even be a good parent? I'm not sure I want children."

"Well, then, damn it, don't have any! See if I care."

"You're angry, aren't you? Sorry, Mom, but I felt I had to spell it out for you."

"And so you have. Happy New Year. Give my love to John. We'll talk soon."

When Meg hung up, she sat down and bawled. Could she do nothing right? She began to wonder if Jack had poisoned Claire against her own mother. He got to see her on a regular basis by virtue of geography, and Meg was lucky if she saw Claire for a few hours once or twice a year. Her gift to Claire had been so well-intentioned! And look how it had been received. Little in life could sting like an adult child's criticism.

Of course her children were entitled to their own lives. Meg had always been the parent who encouraged them to spread their wings. Countless hours spent driving them to music and dance lessons, shopping with friends, school activities – and what had Jack ever done but to expect first Meg and now Claire, and someday probably Jenny, to mother him?

When Meg was Claire's age, Claire had been seven years old, a second grader. If remaining childless was truly Claire's decision, Meg could only hope her daughter wouldn't regret the choice later in life.

She thought of Erin Sumptner and Melody Branscombe, both dead now, leaving no heirs. Perhaps Meg had overrated having children, after all.

Now Claire was furious with her, and Jenny had Owen. And what did she have, other than a job she didn't want, her cats, and a fifteen-year-old dog who refused to die and would probably limp across Meg's grave? No wonder she'd become obsessed with the history of the Hill clan. Only because her own life seemed to have become as barren as Faith Hill's womb.

Snap out of it, Meg; you're a fighter, not a sniveler.

She donned a jacket and mittens and wrapped a scarf around her head. Putting a leash on Cherry Lamb, she jogged out into a twenty-degree, windy day, in a valiant effort to outrun her own self-pitying misery and leave it far behind.

Chapter Twenty-Five

In the last week of January, Meg received a letter from the Richmond law firm of Hirsch and Novicki. The auction had been scheduled for the first Saturday in February, at the Wilson County Courthouse. She carefully scanned the weekly paper for the printed notice of the event that finally appeared only two days before the appointed Saturday, buried in a long listing of classified ads.

The truth was, she no longer wanted the house. But she had told Erin Sumptner she was interested, and before her death Erin had gone to the trouble of putting the wheels in motion. So the least she could do was attend, to be present and accounted for, by whom she had no idea.

On a blustery Saturday, Meg arrived at the courthouse and parked in front on the diagonal, surprised by the few number of shoppers in town. At ten o'clock, a small crowd had gathered for the auction, mostly elderly men attired in the local winter costume of bibbed-overalls, quilted jackets, and billed hats with earflaps. Beneath a green awning from one of the local funeral homes, a church Ladies Auxiliary sold hot cider, coffee, and donuts. Meg bought a cup of coffee, so hot in its Styrofoam cup that she used it to warm her hands. Though the wind had tapered off, a cold drizzle had begun to fall.

And the auctioneer? None other than Ned Roanes, her old real estate agent. He didn't see her standing over by the refreshment stand. But then Meg wondered if he'd recognize her even if he had spotted her in the thin assembly.

"One property to auction off today, Gents! The old Caleb Hill house, located on 862 just outside of the town of Wilson proper. By the authority of a Richmond law firm representing the interests of the final estate.

"The house has five rooms – living room or parlor, dining room, kitchen on the ground floor, two bedrooms upstairs. Built in the last century of oak hand-hewn logs, the house is an excellent example of old-timey Appalachian workmanship. A real collector's item. It sits on one acre of land, with clear, unpolluted springs active the year-round."

Gavel in hand, Ned Roanes stood at the ready. "I'm prepared to receive bids on this unique property."

When no one spoke up, Meg looked around at the faces in the small gathering. Several of the old men seemed embarrassed, or perhaps uncomfortable, she couldn't tell which. There was no mistaking the sudden tension that hung in the air.

"Okay, folks," Ned said with a laugh. "You don't want the house, you can bulldoze it and still have an acre for a prime building site. What am I bid?"

Still, no takers. Then she experienced a weird chill, her eyes pulled magnetically to the outer edge of the group of spectators.

She saw him standing there, hovering invisibly to anyone but Meg Kites, the ghost of Caleb Hill.

"If one of us from Wilson doesn't buy this property," Ned warned, "there's just no telling whose hands it could fall into. Now, I'm getting mighty cold standing up here in the rain. For one last time, gentlemen, what am I bid?"

Reluctantly, Meg raised her arm. "A hundred dollars?"

Smack went Ned's gavel. "Sold! Thank you, Madam."

The rest of the crowd sauntered over to buy refreshments while Meg approached Ned Roanes. "Hi, Ned. Remember me? You sold me a house about this time last year, out on 862. Meg Kites." She shook his puffy hand.

Ned asked her to come into the courthouse and sign the papers. "How do you like your house, Mrs. Kites?"

"Fine, thanks. I've had a little work done on it."

"Say! Doesn't your property border this piece you just bought?"

"Sure does. I couldn't bear it when you suggested the old log house could be torn down. Then I felt as though I just had to buy it."

"Well, you certainly won't be sorry. An acre of land around here these days for a hundred dollars is nearly unheard of."

Signing her full name in several places on various forms, she said, "Why do you think no one else wanted to buy it?"

He looked uneasy. "I don't rightly know."

She stared him in the eye. "Do you think because it's haunted?"

"Aw, now you're pulling my leg!" He couldn't seem to tell whether she might be joking.

Ned was a nice enough fellow, but Meg still remembered he had sold her house to her as is, with no warning, not even a hint about the many items needing repair. "Certainly not. I want you to answer me honestly. After all, I already bought the property, didn't I? I think I'm entitled to know."

"Well, rumor says it is haunted. Of course I don't put much stock in things of that nature."

"You mean ghosts and such."

"People here can be mighty superstitious, Mrs. Kites."

"Among their many other fine attributes, hey, Ned?"

With Meg's check in hand, it didn't take long for Ned Roanes to make his excuses and be on his way.

Meg watched as he hustled to his pick-up truck. She stopped by the refreshment tent and bought a second cup of coffee and a chocolate-frosted donut to take home.

Driving to her house, she told herself that what she had seen at the edge of the crowd was merely hallucination, an imprint from her subconscious projected by her own imagination. Or had he chosen to appear to her a final time, to persuade her to intercede in his behalf and ensure the preservation of his home place?

Hallucination? Meg didn't think so, not that it made much difference. The Caleb Hill house would stand, protected for the moment from the cruel blade of a bulldozer. Now it depended on Meg Kites for safe keeping.

And talk about superstitious! Glancing through her bedroom window that afternoon, since she officially owned the place, for some curious reason she had no desire to go near it. In fact, she did everything possible to push the log house out of her mind.

Wait until Jenny found out what her mother had done!

Later that night, the eerie wailing began, reminding Meg of what the medium Sarah Grimes had said about the banshee, the wailing creature from Irish folklore whose appearance portends death.

Cherry Lamb barked and yelped violently, running around in circles, falling against furniture as if she were having a seizure. Meg went to the back door to let the dog outside, noticing the tranquil calm of the night. Not so much as a gust of wind. And not ten seconds elapsed before Cherry wanted back inside.

In the distance, near the log house, stood a slim pillar of bluish light. As Meg focused on the light, it altered, slowly changing shape, an impressionistic drawing of a woman in a long gown. The apparition drifted from the house to the holly tree, then seemed to turn and gaze at Meg before gliding to the grove of ice-crusted willow trees near the spring. There it hovered, a soft, lavender-blue glow, until it grew dimmer, then dimmer still, and vanished.

She slept poorly, plagued with frightening dreams, and woke up cranky even before she set her bare foot on the cool floor. By God, she would solve this riddle once and for all.

He may think he wants his rest, damn it; but she's the one who needs her rest. This absurd quest into the past had not only disrupted her sleep, but her life...for much too long.

Chapter Twenty-Six

She dressed in her red-wool suit and left the house to attend church services, driving through Burger Master for coffee and an omelet biscuit to eat on the way. The young girl at the window told her Jenny wasn't scheduled to be in until noon.

Perhaps Meg would swing through on her way home from church. But then again, maybe she wouldn't.

The topic of Pastor Smythe's sermon this morning was the vanity of worldly possessions and desires, and the inevitability of the end of the world, taken from Ecclesiastes 12. Those in the congregation who'd brought their dog-eared Bibles turned to follow the passage.

"In the days when the keepers of the house shall tremble, and the strong men shall bow themselves, and the grinders cease because they are few, and those that look out of the windows are darkened....And desire shall fail; because man goeth to his long home, and the mourners go about the streets....Then shall the dust return to the earth as it was, and the spirit shall return unto God, who gave it."

Somehow the natural progression of life into death had been interrupted for Caleb and Lucy. They had not returned to dust, their spirits doomed to wander in eternal torment, unable to rest. Why? What mortal sin had either of them committed, to deserve such a terrible fate?

The small choir assembled on the dais to sing a beautiful hymn that made Meg's eyes well, O, the deep, deep love of Jesus, an old Scottish hymn whose melody flowed relentlessly toward its sad, mournful conclusion, flooding her with an almost intolerable remorse.

How could she have lived her fifty years any differently? She'd done the best she could. If she were to die tomorrow and appeared before the Pearly Gates, she could honestly say she'd lived her life with caring and kindness, and no small measure of integrity.

Then why did she suddenly feel utterly bereft and alone?

Anxious to be outside, in the watery cloud-dimmed sunlight Meg hurried to her car.

The local library was on Main Street. Sunday hours were noon until five p.m. Meg arrived at twelve-fifteen, parked in the lot, and went inside.

She asked the woman at the service counter about accessing the microfiche containing back issues of the Wilson County Monitor.

"The rolls from issues before 1950 are stored away in the back room," the woman said. "Nobody's asked for those in a coon's age. I'll have to find them."

Meg took off her coat and hung it on a nearby coat-rack. She sat down at the machine and waited for the librarian to reappear.

At last she came over with a shoebox. "What years were you interested in, specifically?"

"The year 1897 and everything between until 1916."

The woman placed several canisters on the table. "There you go. Do you know how to operate the machine, and how to rewind when you're finished?"

"It's been a while, but if I need assistance, I'll let you know."

A while, indeed. The last time she'd researched anything through this antiquated method had been in college as an undergraduate, when she'd written a term paper for a class on Post-War European History.

Meg soon discovered that, in his heyday, Lucas Hill had been quite a local celebrity. Again and again, the newspaper recounted stories of his stirring courtroom victories.

Impatient, she changed canisters and went to the year 1906 to find the notice of the memorial service for Caleb Hill, a small paragraph bordered in black.

The year 1905 proved interesting. No notice of Lucy Hill's death, but an article on Lucas Hill's successful prosecution of the spiritualist, Sister Esther Quesenbury, for obtaining money by fraudulent means. No victim was named, but Meg remembered the final pages of Lucy's journal. The midwife Sister Esther had supposedly cast an evil spell on Lucy and prescribed some sort of potion to increase her fertility, with the proviso she spend time each day near the springs to ensure that her next child would also be a son. Had Lucas been compelled to run Sister Esther out of business, after he had witnessed her evil power over Lucy Hill?

Or in a public attempt to discredit her, had he prosecuted the only woman who might have heard the unsavory details from Lucy, implicating Lucas Hill in a sordid event he'd have never wanted to be revealed? When was it that Lucy's second child had been stillborn? Meg found the year 1903. Again, a small paragraph on Baby Ian Hill's funeral, bordered in black.

Meg turned the dial backward, to 1901, fascinated when she saw an announcement of The Amazing Magic Show featuring the magician Caleb Hill and his lovely assistant, Lucinda. An enterprising reporter had interviewed Caleb, whose great feat was stepping into the Siamese Magic Cabinet and disappearing, only to reappear moments later.

A reward was offered to any member of the audience who could explain how the feat had been accomplished. Hungrily, Meg read Caleb Hill's words:

"The cabinet is of my own design and invention. I defy anyone to discover a false door, or any manner whereby I might deceive the audience through cheap trickery or illusion. For when I enter the Siamese Magic Cabinet, I walk through the portal to another dimension not of this earth, an astral body projected into etheric realms."

The standing offer to the successful doubter who proved chicanery was a hundred dollars, a fortune in those days. Caleb Hill must have been very sure of himself.

But what if he really had discovered a crevice between parallel dimensions? What was it Dr. Hollings said?

The Other Now! Andrew Hollings had told Meg about an alternative universe bordering our own, warning that there was always a danger of being sucked over the barrier!

Meg shivered from the thought. Could that possibly have been Caleb's fate? Had he stepped into his cabinet and entered what he called "another dimension not of this earth," and somehow not been able to come back, disappearing forever?

Faith Fleming Hill had written that Caleb had been missing for eight months, and no one knew what had become of him.

Then Meg knew who it had been, the unseen presence directing its wrath against her on a night not so long ago, when she had found a human bite mark on her thigh.

Faith Hill. Her ghost did not want Meg Kites to tamper in paranormal affairs, for the possibility that she might discover the crime her husband had committed against Lucy Hill. She wondered how much of the truth Faith had actually known, what version Lucas Hill had told his wife.

Well, Meg had no sympathy for Faith Hill. Hadn't she claimed Lucy's daughter for her own, denying Melody's true parentage even until the end of Melody's life?

And what kind of woman would live with the knowledge of an offense perpetrated against another woman by her own husband, whatever it was that Lucas had done to Lucy?

Meg returned the box of microfiche canisters to the front desk, understanding she had finally come to the end of the road. She had learned everything there was to know about the Hill family. There were no remaining earthly sources to be consulted.

While driving home, she asked herself, "But if the mystery is solved, why don't I feel a sense of closure?"

Chapter Twenty-Seven

During the last three weeks of February, Meg shed ten pounds without conscious dieting. She'd lost all interest in food, having grown weary of dining alone in front of the evening news, surrounded by her cats and Cherry Lamb.

Claire wrote to say she was sorry for the apparent misunderstanding. Meg replied with a note apologizing for her well-meaning but unwelcome intrusiveness into Claire's life, with a solemn promise never to mention the G word again.

G for grandchild, grandmother, or guilt? Let Claire, an adult woman obviously capable of conducting her own affairs, figure it out for herself.

Jenny called to invite her to come to the trailer for Owen's birthday dinner, but Meg declined. A few times she drove through Burger Master on her way to the office, to say hello to Jenny when Meg knew she was working the breakfast and lunch shift.

At the office, things bumped along monotonously. There was little hope the County Board of Supervisors would approve refilling the welfare fraud investigator position once held by Norman Feder. Meg and Steve Tomazcyk received subpoenas to appear in court, to testify for the insurance company against the couple who'd trashed their Pontiac Cutlass.

One morning Fran Giddings commented to Meg, "You don't seem yourself lately. Is anything wrong?"

"No, nothing's wrong, Fran. Why do you ask?"

"You seem distracted, as if your mind is a million miles from nowhere."

An astute observation, Meg thought to herself. She seemed to be existing in a state of vague expectation. Sitting at her desk over the County Budget Request Package, or driving along in her car with little conscious awareness of traffic patterns, she would suddenly catch herself in a daydream.

Her strange fascination with Caleb Hill had not diminished. Bizarre thoughts came to mind, an image of neon atoms and molecules disintegrating in a black void before reconfiguring as the man she had seen on the country road that morning in September.

Had he actually made his presence known at the auction, compelling Meg to be the only bidder on the Hill property? Would he choose to reappear to her again? Had Caleb and Lucy made a death pact, like Houdini and his wife Bess, that the first to die would contact the one left behind?

Meg continued to visit her little church, steadfastly believing in an Afterlife, sin and retribution. If it were true that at the instant of death the human spirit is sucked through a vortex into a blinding celestial light, what had gone awry with Lucy and then Caleb? During silent prayer, Meg prayed for their tormented souls.

Twice as she happened to be standing on the back porch at twilight, Meg saw the luminescent glow by the willow trees, a bluish, pulsating transparency that slowly dissipated. She understood how such manifestations now seemed ordinary to her. It was the real world that had taken on an eldritch quality, eerie and almost surreal.

A flowering dogwood tree was planted on the courthouse green in memory of Norman Feder. Meg and some of her staff attended, and Marty delivered a weird eulogy about the loss of a dedicated public servant. Meg had to pinch herself to believe it was really happening. No one had been able to tolerate Norm Feder, least of all the County Manager.

Chris Phlegar finally got around to calling Meg, but they had little to say to one another. Their conversation was strained. Meg promised to write, but so far hadn't found the motivation.

Chris was her best friend, and Meg loved her daughters, but this was her own special time, and she didn't want the solitude she seemed to have embraced willingly, even passionately, to come to an end too soon. Going about her prescribed routine, Meg realized one day that she had spent these weeks receptively waiting, anticipating his presence, just as Faith Hill had written in words she probably believed no one would ever read about how she had waited for him while living in this house.

One night, the last day of February, Meg arrived home with an odd premonition that her vigil would not go unrewarded. The cats gobbled their dinner and meowed to be let outside. She left the door ajar and the storm door propped open, but when they came inside, each cat prowled the house, waving his long silky tail back and forth, hissed, and ran outside again.

As she ate dinner, she stared into space with her fork poised midway between her plate and her mouth, startled by a peculiar sensation when an invisible hand slowly stroked her hair.

Calmly, Meg finished the baked potato. Then she called in the cats and locked the door.

Two rooms away, the bathroom door slammed shut. The candles she had lighted for the table guttered, when there was no tangible draft in the room.

She opened her handbag, removed her wallet, and found Sarah Grimes' phone number tucked behind a credit card. Dialing the number, she listened to four rings, thinking Please be home…

"Sarah, this is Meg Kites."

"How's it going with your ghosts? I've thought about you a lot, hoping you might call with an update."

"Well, I bought the old log house for a song. Nobody else bid on it. As the real estate agent reluctantly admitted, local legend claims it's haunted."

"But you said the ghost, or ghosts, seem to respond to you. A simple haunting is merely a spirit anchored to a site for a stretch of years, and may be seen by any number of people. But in a haunting, there's no effort on the part of the spirit to contact the living. It's as if the phantom presence is trapped at a certain place, mindlessly repeating the same action over and over. You told me your experiences have been more personal and animated."

"Animated is a good word. Just a few minutes ago, I was sitting here eating dinner and it felt as though someone stroked my hair. Need I add that I'm here alone?"

"Touch! Very rare. Over three-quarters of visitations are visual. Slightly under half of the people who admit to having seen a spirit also say they heard something. But only a small percentage, maybe less than fifteen per cent, swear to the sense of touch. At least that's what the ghost-research literature reports."

Meg heard the strike and flare of a match over the line. Sarah Grimes was a smoker, too.

"All at once it's seemed to escalate, Sarah. What do you think I should do?"

"Something's trying to communicate, no doubt of it. You have two choices. Move away and avoid it entirely, or tough it out and see what happens next. I doubt whether you're in danger. If there were any malice involved, I'm sure you'd have had some indication by now."

Thinking of the bite on her thigh that subsequently vanished, Meg tried to joke, "Do you make house calls?"

"If I come to your house, all will be quiet. It's not me he wants, Meg. It's you. For some reason, only you."

"I don't know why, but I'm not at all frightened. Just interested, as you said, in what happens next."

"How are your cats?"

"Skittish and jumpy. But now they're lying around peacefully."

"Cats are a good barometer. They can verify when something you can't see may be near."

Meg sighed, suddenly annoyed by the whole thing, and especially of not being in control of forthcoming events. "I'm not sure, Sarah, but I may need to consult with you again."

"Please let me know what happens. I'm almost always here after six."

Over the next days, doors opened when Meg was certain they had been shut, or closed when she knew she'd left them open. One night while she was in bed she heard footsteps, as if someone walked slowly through her house.

Sweet Babu, her taffy cat, slept on a pillow beside her bed, and sometimes he reared up curiously and stared for a long moment before curling into a ball to settle down. He was the only one of her cats who seemed to know instinctively, as Meg did, that the presence in the house was not threatening and meant no harm.

Suddenly she began to crave sleep, retiring earlier each night for vivid dreams she couldn't remember. When she awoke in the morning, she felt refreshed, as if protective arms had comforted her during the night as she slept. For the first time in memory, she felt safe.

Several times Meg considered using the Ouija board to try and communicate with Caleb, but for the fact that she had no assurance a more hostile spirit might not get through. Thinking of the teeth marks, she suspected she'd be inviting danger by resorting to the Ouija even a last time.

Dr. Hollings had been accurate in saying the American movies had given the Ouija board bad press. Her memory of terrifying scenes from *The Exorcist* served as a reminder that consulting the Ouija was simply too unpredictable and risky.

One night an ice storm covered the blanket of snow. The wind spit sleet against the windows. At eleven o'clock Meg listened to the weather report on WDBJ-TV from Roanoke, to hear that all government offices, schools, and many businesses in the area would be closed in the morning due to treacherous road conditions. Already, dozens of accidents had been reported, and two people had died.

Then the lights flickered on and off, and the power went out. She piled extra blankets on the bed and went to sleep.

Other than the times she got up blearily to feed the cats or let out the dog, to use the bathroom or get a sip of water for her dry mouth, Meg slept for two nights and a day. Jenny's call roused her from bed.

"I've been calling and calling! Where have you been, Mom? Are you okay?"

"No, I think I had the flu. I'm better now. I've been asleep."

"We're staying in town at Brianna's parents' house. They have a generator. Our power is still out at the trailer. At Burger Master, too. All over town."

Just then Meg's lights came on, and the furnace and water pump began to hum.

"Tomorrow it's supposed to warm up. I heard it on the radio. And believe it or not, the power's been restored here."

"Thank Heaven! Mom, are you sure you'll be all right?"

"No, to be honest. Something's been on my mind. But I'll get over it. Have you talked with Claire?"

After the ice came the rain blown in by westerly winds. March brought the great thaw, flooding streams and back roads and closing Wilson County schools for a week.

Meg felt as if she'd been frozen in a block of ice, unable to move since she bought the Caleb Hill house, as though she'd fallen under a spell. Spring couldn't come quickly enough to suit her. She looked forward to cultivating dirt with a trowel, and planting onion sets and lettuce and spinach seeds in the backyard garden patch.

On Saturday she carried in a large cardboard box from the grocery store and set it in the middle of the kitchen floor. She'd decided to rid herself of any reminder of the Hill clan, beginning with the Ouija board, Faith's papers, her own notes and Hill chronology, even the antique amethyst and diamond ring, extricating herself from the last vestiges of her obsession.

Meg couldn't bring herself to destroy such personal remnants of other lives, but neither did she want them in her home. Sadly, she found Lucy's gardening journal and tossed it in, together with the missing pages she'd found in the woodstove. Last were the photographs of Caleb at his son's funeral, and of Lucy astride the Victor bicycle wearing a long gabardine skirt, a high-necked blouse, and a roguish smile.

After securely tucking the flaps and taping them shut, she delivered the box to the porch of the log house. Unlocking the door, she slid the box into the house, where it seemed out of place. She decided to carry it upstairs, to store in one of the bedrooms.

Again, Lucy's regal portrait stared at her from the top of the stairs, a lovely red-haired Irish lass in a brown-velvet wedding gown, the marriage bouquet in her hands described in the gardening journal as orange blossoms and gardenias.

"I'm finished with you, Lucy Hill," she said. "Here are your things."

She glanced for a last time at the bicycle propped against the wall, at the Irish harp and ballerina slippers, at the silver-plated chest on Lucy's vanity table containing the locket forever preserving the single strand of a baby's hair.

As she turned to descend the stairs, Meg was gripped by a sensation of panic. Her arms were gooseflesh, her knees trembled. Suddenly she wanted nothing more than to be out of this house.

A violent blow to her stomach almost caused her to lose her balance, but she held onto the banister, trying to catch her breath. Dear Lord, had she had a heart attack? Weakly, she climbed the top step and slumped to the landing, breathing rapidly as she struggled to pump air into her lungs, her thoughts reeling.

The terror-stricken woman Meg recognized as Lucy Hill clutched an infant to her chest. Her red hair jutted from her head in a disheveled halo, she wore a long white gown. She stood beside Meg on the landing and looked down the stairs at a short, brawny, balding man stomping toward her.

You'll not have this infant, Lucas!

The child is dead. I must bury it before Caleb sees...damn you, woman. Give me the child!

Horrified, Meg watched as Lucas Hill pushed Lucy against her own portrait, as he ripped the infant from her arms.

Lucy screamed, pummeling his head, his shoulders with her small fists, screaming and crying that the baby was hers, and she would never let him have it.

May the Almighty strike me dead before you take my child, Lucas Hill. I'll tell your wife what you did to me! I shall!

You'll do nothing of the sort. You're mad! Everyone knows it, even Caleb suspects you're stark raving mad!

And then, with one strong blow, he struck her in the face. She fell, screaming. Like a rag doll, head over heels, Lucy tumbled down the stairs.

Meg blinked, shaking her head as if coming out of a daze. The stairs were empty. She was alone on the landing.

The painted smile of Lucy Hill's wedding portrait captured in oil for all eternity seemed triumphant.

Even Meg knew she hadn't dreamed it. She had experienced retrocognition, the past slipping into the present, just as unmistakably real as when the incident had occurred, though this time Meg Kites had been a silent, unseen witness.

Now, at last, she knew. Lucas Hill had raped his own brother's wife, and when she had given birth to his child, he had murdered Lucy Hill.

Chapter Twenty-Eight

The violent storms of March blended with an April that began with warm rains and mellowed into days of early spring sunshine.

While the earth was still soggy, a back-hoe operator drove his rig up a cattle trail bordering the meadow in front of the Hill house. Meg waited for him at the site selected by the environmental inspector from the public health department as good drainage for the septic system. Today the hole would be dug, the tank sunk and covered over.

Next week two local men were scheduled to install the water pipes for running water to the log house from the springs. Mid-summer, the bathroom would be constructed off the kitchen.

In the fall, she'd have the house wired for electricity, a furnace put in, and some of the interior walls re-plastered. Though she didn't relish the thought, to save money, Meg planned to do the painting herself, an ongoing project to occupy herself on long winter weekends.

If all went according to plan, she could rent out the house by next March, and recoup her five-thousand-dollar investment in a few years. Then, aside from annual property taxes and homeowner's insurance, she'd have a tidy source of revenue for her retirement years.

The site for the septic tank had been roped off. After a few words to the man on the back-hoe, Meg sat on the front porch of the old house, to observe.

Before the back-hoe had finished its work, a flatbed drove up with the concrete tank. Three men in baseball caps got out of the cab of the truck and went to talk with the back-hoe driver. Apparently, they were all on a first-name basis.

The moment her eyes fell upon the cairn, Meg knew it had always been there. Before the snows came, she had noticed it before, thinking some farmer had cleared the land years ago, piling the rocks at the edge of the meadow on a slight hill overlooking the springs surrounded by willow trees.

A cairn of rocks in the meadow.

Slowly she walked to the rocks and touched them. Then she jogged across the field to the four men, who were preparing to lift the tank with chains attached to the flatbed's crane and lower it into the ground.

"I'm sorry, but I need you to dig something over here."

"We're fixin' to unload the septic tank."

"Well, I know, and I want you to." She directed her remarks to the back-hoe driver. "Could you get this machine onto that little knoll, just beyond the springs?"

"Well, sure, if I run her up sideways."

"Could you do it now?"

The man glanced at the other men, exchanging a wry, working-man's glance that said Women! "Okay, I guess so. But what am I digging for?"

"I don't...I have a hunch, and...I'll pay you extra for your time."

"It's sixty-five an hour, Ma'am."

"This won't take but a few minutes, I'm almost positive."

Shortly, the man had jockeyed the machine onto the slight crest of the hill, directly beneath the cairn as Meg had requested. And it didn't take an hour, but only ten minutes and several hefty swipes of the back-hoe until the bucket clanged against a solid obstruction.

Meg watched as he hopped off the machine and stood at the edge of the four-foot hole, then lowered himself down into it.

"Seems like I hit rock, or something," he shouted to her. After a few seconds more, he climbed up to ground level and said, "Jesus, lady. Looks like there's somebody buried here."

"What do we do now?"

The man scratched the back of his head. "Tell you the truth, I don't rightly know."

"Well, just wait here a minute, would you? I have to phone someone."

She ran back to her house and called the veterinary clinic.

Fortunately, it was only eleven-thirty, and on Saturdays he was always there until noon.

"Vet's office," Cole Mitchum said.

"Dr. Mitchum, this is Meg Kites. Who has to be present to exhume an unmarked grave? I've just discovered one on the property in back of my house."

"Medical examiner, usually. But the Sheriff will do in a pinch. I'll call him and we'll be out. You said you're on 862 in Faith Hill's old place, didn't you?"

True to his word, Cole Mitchum's Jeep followed the Sheriff's Crown Victoria to Meg's house within half an hour. Then they were standing around the hole, six men and Meg Kites.

"Who's going to do the honors?" the back-hoe driver said.

"Hell, I'll do it," the vet said. "Any of you men have something I can use to jimmy the front of this casket off?" One of the men ran back to the flat-bed.

"I'll help you," Sheriff Granger said. "Cole, your heart could plum give out, old fart like you. Wouldn't want that on my conscience."

Dr. Mitchum chuckled, as did the other men, at the Sheriff's attempt at levity in the face of the profane act they were driven to perform.

Meg stood off at a slight distance, listening as the steel bar clanged against metal and splintered wood, as the Sheriff and Cole Mitchum grunted from their exertion. The first robin of spring lighted on a branch of a willow tree and called to its mate, a sign for Meg that life persists in an ever-winding cycle of birth and renewal, of hope.

"We got it loose!" the Sheriff said. "Donnie, get over here and take a hold on the other end."

In a denim skirt, a plaid blouse, and a white sweater, Meg felt chilled to the bone when she heard the groan of the lid being lifted. She pulled the sweater together at her throat.

"Saints preserve us," Cole Mitchum said. "It's Lucy Hill."

The Sheriff whistled. "Cole, how long would you reckon she's been dead?"

"She died in 1905," Meg called to them.

"Well, shoot!" Sheriff Granger said. "Looks like she was put down here yesterday, just about."

Meg started to go to the grave and see for herself, but decided against it. "Dr. Mitchum, is there a baby with her?"

"Yep. A poor, shriveled little thing she was holding in her arms. Deformed. You know, I've never seen anything like it. Except for one little piece of skin missing on Lucy's right cheek, she looks so natural you'd almost think she was sleeping. I'll have to get the medical examiner to verify it, but slow disintegration of a corpse usually means arsenic poisoning."

"Shooo!" one of the men from the flatbed said, swabbing his forehead with a red bandana. Meg noticed that each of the men had removed his baseball cap.

With a hand from the Sheriff, the veterinarian hoisted himself from the grave and started giving instructions. "Donnie, dig this out some more and, after you've sunk the tank, load this casket onto the flatbed and we'll take her to town. Poor woman deserves a proper burial. Meg, I'll need to use your telephone."

Donnie climbed onto the back-hoe and began to dig, while the other three men completed the task of installing the septic tank. Sheriff Granger and Dr. Mitchum followed Meg to her house. She poured three cups of coffee while Cole Mitchum placed the call to a local funeral home.

Accepting his coffee from Meg, Sheriff Granger said, "Thanks. But I swan, if the woman buried up there in that pasture all these years don't beat all. Never seen nothing like it."

Dr. Mitchum joined them at the table, spooning sugar into his coffee. "Willard says he'll be at the funeral home in an hour to meet the medical examiner driving in from Roanoke. He needs us to sign the papers as witnesses to the exhumation. Arsenic poisoning, when we thought she'd just up and left town, maybe gone back to Ireland."

"I found part of her diary in the old house out back," Meg said. "According to Lucy's own words, evidently the child she bore and was buried with wasn't her husband Caleb's, but Lucas Hill's. She wrote that he was giving her quinine. But it wasn't quinine, was it?"

The vet shook his head. "Sometimes it's best not to dig up the past. Lucas lived to a ripe old age, with what he might have done pressing on his conscience." He paused to slurp several sips of coffee. "If he was guilty of what you're accusing him of, I'd wager that a thousand times he wished he could have changed places with her in the grave, to end his torment."

Sheriff Granger nodded and said, "Why else did he hire a sin-eater?"

"A sin-eater?" Meg said. "What on earth is that?"

The Sheriff stared at her. "Well, you must not be from Wilson or any of these parts. That's old-timey mountain folklore. You hire some-body to eat a piece of the dead person's skin, to save his soul from Hell."

"My God! How barbaric!"

"Just depends on how you're raised up, I reckon," the Sheriff re-plied, a trifle defensively.

Anxious to change the subject, she asked, "When will you bury her, Sheriff?"

"If Willard can stick around, we'll do it before supper."

Meg looked at the two men. "I'd like to be there."

Cole Mitchum placed his coffee mug in the sink. "Well, guess we better get out there and see how far along they are, getting that casket free."

Meg grabbed her checkbook and went with them. Two men had chained the casket to the flatbed. The back-hoe driver had filled in the grave, and was almost finished covering the septic tank. The flatbed left, Cole Mitchum and the Sheriff following behind, in what Meg thought of as Lucy Hill's belated funeral procession.

She waited for Donnie on the front porch. He drove the back-hoe close to the old house and got down to walk toward the porch, his base-ball cap in hand.

"No extra for the last, Ma'am. Couldn't take money for something needed bein' done."

As she turned to go to her house, she noticed the red tulips and purple crocus she'd planted at the side of the log house, green tips jutting through the soft earth and soon to bloom.

Again, the robin sang.

This time, there was an answer.

****

Lucy Hill was interred that April afternoon beside her husband's grave in the cemetery on the knoll overlooking the town, with Sheriff Granger, Cole Mitchum, Meg Kites, Willard Samuels, and Pastor Smythe in attendance. Meg arranged to have a local man engrave the year of Lucy's death on the monument shared with Caleb and Baby Ian.

As they were leaving the grave site and walking to their cars, Meg asked her minister if he'd been able to find the special prayer she'd requested, when she telephoned earlier to request his presence at the cemetery.

He nodded. "I found it in an old book in my study. It's dated 1631, and while I don't believe it was ever an official part of the Catholic liturgy, there's a reason it was written in a time when evil was considered real, when people truly feared Satan and his legions."

She smiled. "Not like us nonbelievers today, eh?"

"You believe, Meg. If you didn't, you'd never have asked me for such a prayer."

"Would you mind stopping by the old house for a few minutes and saying the prayer for me? I suppose I could recite it myself, but I'd feel better if you'd do it."

"I'll follow you to your house, then."

The sun was low in the sky as Meg and her pastor bowed their heads in the living room of the Caleb Hill house. Pastor Smythe's deep voice resonated in the silence.

"Let us pray. 'Do Thou, O Lord, enter graciously into the home that belongs to Thee. Construct for Thyself an abiding resting-place in the hearts of Thy faithful servants, and grant that in this house no wickedness or malicious spirits may ever hold sway. We ask this in the name of our precious Lord and Savior Jesus Christ, king of the world now and forever more. Amen.'"

"Thank you," Meg said. She felt at peace, sensing that the

wandering spirits of Caleb and Lucy Hill had been released. At last, Caleb Hill had found his final rest.

As she walked her minister to his Dodge Caravan, he asked, "And may I look forward to seeing you for Sunday service at church tomorrow?"

She laughed. "You got me! Yes, I'll be there."

Climbing behind the wheel to drive away, he said, "We're having a potluck after the service, Meg, and I do believe we're short a dessert." Pastor Smythe's sweet-tooth was legend.

"I'll bring my famous cherry-chocolate cheesecake," she said with a grin. "You're going to love it."

Chapter Twenty-Nine

After church on Sunday, while awaiting delivery of a cord of green firewood, Meg called Chris Phlegar and Sarah Grimes to tie up the loose ends of the Hill family mystery. She planned to telephone Andrew Hollings during the week, the last person she felt should know of the outcome of her experiences with the Hill house. Oh, and Ted Rucker, of course. She couldn't wait to fill Ted in on Monday.

Jenny had called last night to ask Meg to make a double batch of her special Italian potato soup. Jenny said she just had a taste for it, but Meg surmised that money was probably a little tight, and she wanted some to take home to the trailer.

By four o'clock, the soup simmered in a large kettle on the stove. When the oven timer rang, Meg removed two jelly-roll pans with a double batch of broccoli and cheese bierrocks, a savory filling wrapped like dumplings in a flaky, whole-wheat crust. Jenny loved those, too, split open warm from the oven and slathered with sour cream.

A sharp knock at the front door. Meg went to answer, glad that the wood had arrived before dark.

He was a big, muscular, blond, blue-eyed country man with a gentle smile. "Are you Meg Kites? I'm Duncan Flinchum. Your wood's out on the truck."

Hmmm, no baseball cap, she thought to herself as she opened the door. "Come in, Duncan. I'll find my gloves and help you stack it."

The big man stood awkwardly in her kitchen, trying without success to keep his eyes away from the cooling bierrocks and the steaming kettle of soup. "Something smells mighty good."

"Well, you're welcome to it, but your wife is probably waiting dinner."

"Nope. I'm a two-time loser. The second wife made an appointment at the hairdresser's and never came home. That was about a year ago."

"Duncan, have a seat."

Over two giant bowls of soup and four bierrocks, Meg learned of Duncan's history, and told him the high points of hers. She suspected that, between the two of them, they could craft the lyrics of another country song. Just call it Heartbreak.

She believed he was the most honest and open man she'd ever met. Her cats liked him, too. Babu went so far as to hop up on the table and sample Duncan's soup from the bowl, which made him laugh.

"Sorry," she said, setting the cat on the floor.

"That's all right. I'm real fond of critters."

"You are? Don't you have any bad habits? Do you drink?"

"Nope. Don't smoke, neither. Never did."

"There must be something you're not telling me. I'm trying to figure out why two wives would leave you when you seem like such a nice man."

"I had triple by-pass surgery four years ago. Since you just buried a man you cared for, I thought I should be up-front with you."

"Why? Are you planning to bring me some more wood?" Meg meant it as a joke, but as she could see by his confused expression, he didn't know how to take it.

"I'd like to see you again, sure I would. You're easy to talk to. And the food was delicious."

"I like to cook."

"And I like to eat. How's that for a match made in Heaven?"

Meg laughed. "Come on, Duncan, before we lose the light. I'll help you unload."

As he followed her out the door, she looked back at him and grinned. Duncan Flinchum's daughter was a year older than Claire, his son three years younger. And he was fifty-one.

For twenty minutes she handed lengths of wood to him off the truck and he stacked it neatly at the back of her house near the door to the basement. He worked methodically, obviously a man with patience to burn.

And he was a big eater and didn't watch his diet, most likely. She thought about her recipes for appetizing low-fat dishes as a harmless way to assuage her caretaker personality.

"Duncan, can you actually make a living with wood delivery?" Meg asked.

"Right smart. Cleared fifty thousand some years ago after I paid my men, when I had four trucks going before my heart attack. In the summer I mow lawns. There's money in it, too. And I paint houses, if'n a job comes up. Real reasonable. Sixty dollars a room."

"Do you?"

When they were finished unloading the wood, Meg said, "Duncan, would you mind taking a look at my woodstove and teach me how to keep a fire burning in it? I'm afraid I don't have anyone else to ask except you."

"You're not seeing somebody?" he said, his surprised expression a compliment in itself to a fifty-year-old woman with a dark-brown rinse.

She led him down the stairs to the basement for a lesson in building a fire in a woodstove. Cherry Lamb had developed a shine for Duncan, and he waited until the old dog limped down the stairs, making sure she could arrive safely.

"She's a sweet old thing," he said, gently stroking behind the dog's ears, bringing up whimpers of contentment.

You will do, Duncan Flinchum, Meg thought to herself. Yes, you'll do nicely.